WIZARD'S GUILD

VOLUME 5

THE GREAT FORGET FANTASY SERIES

TERRY IRONWOOD

All rights reserved. No part of this publication may be reproduced, stored or transmitted in any form or by any means, electronic, mechanical, photocopying, recording, scanning, or otherwise without written permission from the publisher. It is illegal to copy this book, post it to a website, or distribute it by any other means without permission.

COPYRIGHT © 2024 by Terry Ironwood

THIS NOVEL IS ENTIRELY a work of fiction. The names, characters and incidents portrayed in it are the work of the author's imagination. Any resemblance to actual persons, living or dead, events or localities is entirely coincidental.

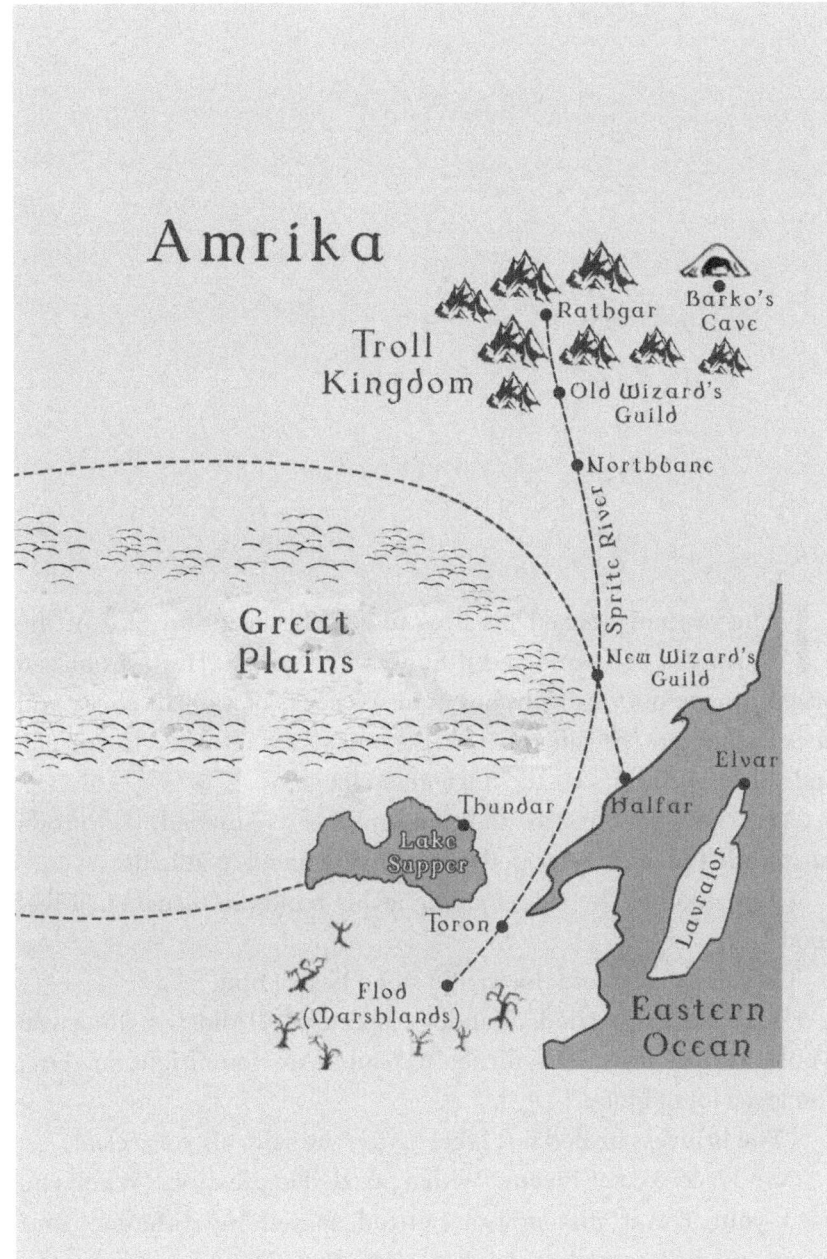

1

The orphan opened his eyes to see the beautiful face of the princess. He wondered if he was in a dream. Her eyes blazed bright brown, but strangely, he could see flecks of red. His cheek and neck itched but felt much better. Eleanor's eyes returned to normal, and she hugged him. He did not want to let go.

The boy sat up to look around and groaned. Cornrows surrounded them. He decided that he really hated cornfields.

Chip stood to the side, looking at his hands in disbelief. "I feel good."

Captain Melvin and the wizard stood beside him.

"You had us worried," Xander responded, "I did not think you would heal that fast." He turned to Chip. "Are you alright, my boy? You lost a lot of blood."

"The princess healed me. I feel better," he said, his voice clear.

Xander looked at Eleanor with a puzzled expression. "When you used your Power just now, I noticed something different. Your brown magic seemed to have a... red hue. Does that make any sense?"

She started nodding, "Yes... I feel different too, more powerful. It is hard to explain, and I do not know why." She looked at Chip.

"When you healed me, I felt something... Your blood dripped on me and..." She gasped.

"I saw red spots in your eyes," he said, eyes widening. "I think somehow you now have bits of the Red Level in you."

The wizard's mouth hung open. "I have never heard of such a thing. How fascinating."

"I have it too," Chase added, still looking at his hands. "I am stronger, better."

"Are you saying you have magic?" Xander asked incredulously.

"Huh?" Chase gave the wizard a look normally reserved for him. "No, I don't think so. I feel... improved. My senses too." He picked up a dagger amidst the bodies, shrugged, and sliced his skin. Nothing happened. He sliced much harder, and only a faint line appeared. Garth's eyes widened.

"Chase, come here," the princess ordered. He walked over to her, and she looked into his eyes. "You do have it! Your blue eyes have red bits!"

Xander looked at Chip, calculating. He nodded. "It is your blood, boy. You bled on them and used your blood to replenish theirs. It seems you have increased Eleanor's Power and Chase's physical attributes." He laughed, looking at the sky. "The wizards have been trying to increase their Protector's strength and longevity for millennia. Any effects were short-lived, such as imbuing a shield temporarily with magic. Balor will find this quite interesting. Do you feel different?"

Chip shook his head. He broke through the Wall, seizing his Power. He was still physically weak from blood loss, but his magic felt the same. He reached out with his mind, seeing what life forms were still alive in the cornfields. He especially wanted to make sure Silvermane was safe. The boy could sense nothing in the area. He released his hold on the Power and looked at the wizard.

"I am tired, but my Power is the same."

"Even better. I thought for a moment they had gained at your loss. This needs further study. The question is whether the other Levels can achieve the same result. I suspect the connection to the person receiving the healing is important too." Xander turned to Captain Melvin. "After Chip passed out, I surveyed the area with my Power. All your guards are dead. I am sorry. There may still be a Dark Elf about who controlled these demons, but I sense no one. Stay alert. Let's gather what supplies we can find and see if any horses that ran off survived." Melvin nodded, saluting.

Chip began walking in the direction where the wolf and wasp demon disappeared. It was not difficult to follow. Corn stalks were crushed in a zigzag line. Eleanor saw the concern on his face and joined him. The wizard also stopped talking and signalled for the others to follow.

The boy began to see patches of red and black blood as he followed the twisting trail of broken corn. His apprehension grew as the amount of blood increased. A great struggle was waged here. In the end, his fears were realized. Chip saw a large gray and silver body lying on its side, unmoving.

"No," he whispered, approaching the huge animal. The others gave him space.

Silvermane was on his side, eyes open, forever gazing at nothing. The mountain wolf's once beautiful, shaggy mane was matted with blood. His stomach and throat were torn open. A large hole was visible where his heart would be. The dog's brown eyes were dead and unseeing.

Chip sank to his knees beside the great body, laying his hand on a clean patch of fur. Tears welled unbidden to his eyes. He felt like he had lost a friend, one who had warned him of danger and, in the end, saved his life. The noble animal kept true to his word until the very end. Tears rolled down the boy's cheeks. The orphan had struggled for a long time, not only in the last few weeks but since his birth. Chip had fought his heart out, yet Silvermane was dead. He wept, angry at the unfairness of it all. The boy broke through the Wall and drew in his Power. The others looked at him with compassion, not daring to intervene.

The orphan bathed the dog in his magic, removing the blood and repairing the animal's wounds. The coat shimmered beautifully, and the great mountain wolf lifted into the air, resplendent even in death. Using his Power, Chip swiped his hand in one motion, scooping out a large mound of earth and corn. He slowly lowered the gallant animal into the grave, then closed the great dog's eyes.

The boy stood up and looked down for the last time at Silvermane, King of the Mountain Wolves. He bent, bowing low in homage to the honourable creature. The others did the same. Using his magic, the orphan filled the grave with earth.

"Xander," Chip said, his eyes wet, "which way to the Guild?" The wizard pointed to the right. "Stand out of the way," he ordered. The rest of them nodded, stepping to the side. The boy raised his hands and sent his presence out, sensing for life. There was none.

Unleashing his rage, Chip sent a wall of red fire forward, incinerating the rows of corn plants in a wide swath until the fields ended. Xander's eyes widened. The way ahead of them was cleared for five hundred feet. The boy dropped his hands. "I will not be caught off guard again." He began walking towards the Guild. "I will wait for you at the edge of the field. I want to be alone."

Chip strode forward by himself, the others respecting his grief. The dark clouds overhead finally opened with a crack of thunder, and sheets of rain came pouring down as if the very sky was weeping at the passing of the great Silvermane.

The companions searched the area, picking up their belongings, and luckily found two supply horses that had decided to come back. They slung anything salvageable over their backs. There were too many pieces of the other guards to bury, so Xander decided to say a prayer to the Creator and cremate them with his magic. The rain made the task uncomfortable but washed away the ashes, cleansing the whole area. He left the demon bodies as evidence of how far their reach extended. When finished, they walked down the scorched, open area and reunited with the Guardian.

Chip turned when they approached, feeling more at peace with himself. Xander nodded in approval. "Glad to see your spirits have improved. We have suffered great losses today."

"I take responsibility," said the weapons master. "I lead us into an environment we were untrained for, including myself. The tracker demons were in their element in these cornfields. They can move with stealth and sense by smell alone. We were easy targets, out of our comfort zone."

"I take responsibility as well," Captain Melvin stated. "It was my job to provide protection."

"I did not see it either," Xander admitted. "The cornfields restrained our magic because we feared striking our own. Visually, the plants blinded us, allowing little room for maneuvering. We are lucky to make it out alive. That wasp demon was the worst I have seen. The black blood near the mountain wolf indicates it has wounds. With luck on our side, it may crawl away and die, but I prefer to prepare for the worst. Once healed, it will be a fearsome foe. The wasp's armour withstood some of my magic and our blades. Its speed was terrifying. I do not know if it can fly, but that would be even more disturbing. We are now on foot, which will take longer. We need to reach the Guild before it heals and attacks again."

"Let it try," Chip said quietly. "I welcome it."

The wizard looked at him, narrowing his eyes. "Careful not to tempt fate."

"I tempt it!" The boy whirled with clenched fists. "Silvermane will not die in vain. I will kill that demon insect, one way or another." He strode off, heading east through the rain. The wizard shared a look with the weapons master, who said nothing. They followed the Guardian.

FAR TO THE WEST, Queen Charlotte gazed out the window of the tallest tower in Vanalon. Before her, pouring through the gates, was a vast demon army, thousands strong, commanded by three Inner Circle. The Calgar forces, including the queen, had made a terrible mistake.

At first sight of the demons massing in the valley, they evacuated the city. The Inner Circle members, however, were cunning. Over the past few weeks, they had slowly built a sizable force east of the city to cut off escape, a few at a time, in the dead of night. The sentries had not noticed the slow buildup until three hundred strong blocked the One Road.

When the main demon army came thundering into the valley, the humans tried to flee but were thwarted by the smaller army lying in wait.

The queen had sent Miss Owl and her personal guards, Marcus and Gavin, ahead with a large contingent of arms to try and break through the demon ranks while she and Captain Peters brought up the rear. The front army fought valiantly and opened a hole large enough to slip through before the main demon horde arrived. Unfortunately, the Calgar forces were cut in two. The back half had no choice but to retreat to the city.

With only five hundred men left, they manned the walls as best they could. The Inner Circle quickly disposed of the magic wielders, Miriam and the two Yellows, dressed in blue robes, before smashing the gates.

With nowhere to go, the Calgars switched strategies from escape to taking out as many demons as possible before succumbing to the inevitable. It was a heroic effort, even with the gates gone. The traps out front and the boiling pitch killed hundreds of demons, but they had to retreat to the palace walls.

From there, the Inner Circle easily smashed the smaller iron gates, sending them careening into a dozen soldiers, ending their lives. The surviving men fell back to the palace, barring the doors to little effect. The escape route under the throne had been compromised long before the attack. When they lifted the trap door, it was full of demons. They were barely able to close it.

Morgo must have sent a demon back to inform the Unnamed One of the tunnel when he first discovered it, one last parting gift from the general.

The remaining soldiers fought bravely until the lead Inner Circle member, a thin, skeletal female Dark Elf, entered and incinerated all combatants in the front hall. She killed demons and soldiers alike, without compunction, using her blue fire.

In the throne room, Queen Charlotte had shared a look with Captain Peters and then ran out the back door towards the tower. He remained behind, accepting his fate. The queen had almost delayed too long, not realizing the foul creatures had already infiltrated the halls. Several demons blocked her way, but she sent lancing yellow fire into their eyes, killing them.

When she reached the entrance to the tower stairs, the queen did not notice the spider-like demon crawling through the hall window behind her. As she opened the door, it leapt on her, slicing her back to the bone. Charlotte managed to turn around and send the last of her small magic into its face. It was not enough to kill the beast, but it allowed her to run up the stairs, blood dripping off her dress. The half-mutilated spider demon followed her, shrieking through its burnt mouth. Exhausted, she reached the top of the stairs just as it caught up to her. One of its forelegs raked her again, drawing fresh blood, but she managed to slide through the door and lock it.

Now, she stared out the window, watching the foul demons crawl over her beautiful city. There were so many of them. She turned, her breath ragged, and stumbled over to the writing desk. The queen scribbled a note. Blood dripped from her wounds. Banging and clawing sounded on the wooden door. More demons had arrived on the other side, shrieking with the anticipation of tearing into her human flesh. They knew she was trapped.

The hinges on the door began to buckle, and the center cracked. She finished the message and tied it to the leg of her favourite pigeon.

The door suddenly burst open, and a chorus of shrieks sounded as the demons poured through.

Holding the pigeon with two hands, the queen ran to the open window. Even as she did, the demons in the front crashed into her back. The force carried her completely through the top window of the tower, and she sailed through the air, finally able to release the bird. Several demons flew out with her, still trying to claw at her skin as they plummeted to their deaths. Queen Charlotte of Vanalon spread her arms wide as she took in the beautiful horizon one last time.

THE COMPANIONS ENCOUNTERED several more cornfields but each time went around. None of them cared to repeat their recent experience. The rain poured steadily for a few hours but ceased by mid-afternoon as the dark clouds moved south. They ate some cheese and bread, not stopping. Garth held the reigns of the supply horses.

The sun began to set behind them as they finally reached the foothills. Small clusters of trees appeared, and green grass returned. After weeks of wheat fields, they welcomed the respite. The weapons master urged them on until they found a thicker group of trees that shielded them from the elements. They refilled their water skins in a nearby stream and set up the only two tents they had left. Garth deemed a fire too risky given the threat of the wasp demon returning and the possibility of a Dark Elf nearby. They changed into whatever dry clothes were available, hanging the wet ones on a line they tied between two trees.

Chip felt exhausted and settled down without speaking. The weapons master took the first watch and Captain Melvin the second, rotating through.

Thoughts of Silvermane invaded the boy's mind, causing him to toss and turn. He replayed the events repeatedly, wishing the end would change. What soothed him was one of Garth's sayings, "Learn from the past and move on. It cannot be changed."

To everyone's relief, morning arrived without incident, and the boy awoke rested, if not refreshed. They broke camp and continued walking eastward, following the faint trail. The rolling hills became more extensive, and beautiful green meadows appeared between them. Chip watched as orange and yellow butterflies danced above long green grass. It reminded him of the foothills east of Cave Mountain. The sky was bright blue without a cloud in sight.

The memory of the cornfields and Silvermane's death began to recede, and he opened his mind to the beauty of nature.

The princess walked beside him, and he started talking again, commenting on the scenery. Seeing his spirits rise made her smile, and she clasped his hand. The boy glanced at her as they walked, thanking the Creator that she was still with him. He hoped the prophecy was foiled and she would not die after all.

Perhaps, by increasing her Power through his blood, her old self had in a sense died, fulfilling the prophecy. He would ask the wizard if it was possible when the time was right. For now, he would enjoy her company.

By early afternoon, they reached a babbling brook and stopped for lunch. Garth handed out cured meat and cheese. Chase ate happily, making strange comfort noises. The princess looked at Chip, trying not to giggle. He could not help smiling in return.

Xander swallowed a piece of meat, looking eastward. "We will reach the Ancient Woods by late afternoon. The great trees were planted three millennia ago when the fortress was built. The Wizard's Guild had to be relocated after the Troll King Jaggar forced my brother Balor to abandon it. Jaggar believed he should have been elected High Mage of the Council after we erected the barrier.

"Balor felt that Arkan's sacrifice gave him the right to carry on as High Wizard in his father's place. In the end, my brother decided a vote was not required. The council fragmented and split into factions.

"Upon hearing of the impending attack on the Guild by Jaggar's troll army, many deserted, weary of fighting. At the time, even the High King of Toron would not come to Balor's aid, given his losses sustained in the Great Battle. My brother had no choice but to abandon the fortress. He took what histories he could carry and emptied the treasury. It was said he had more wealth than all the kingdoms combined. Balor built the Guild a day's ride east of us, in a rare spot surrounded on all sides by rivers. The Ancient Woods were created at the same time, using seeds acquired from the great trees in Fang Forest. The fortress itself took a century to complete. My brother spared no expense. He felt that the sheer grandeur of the place would ensure a continued reverence and respect for his legacy. When completed, High Wizard Balor invited the kings and queens of all Amrika to celebrate the opening ceremony. There, he established binding oaths and contracts for humans and wizards to protect each other for all time. A hefty tithe or tax was founded, paid by each city, to support the upkeep of the fortress, train magic wielders, advise the monarchs, and protect the race of humankind from all enemies. My brother may have deep flaws, but he did create a Wizard's Guild for the ages."

"What are his flaws?" Chase asked mid-chew.

"My brother is arrogant, overconfident, self-entitled, controlling, and demanding. He rarely listens to other's opinions and relies on prophecy when it suits him. He tolerates the High Seer Skylar, generally taking his words as fact, yet interprets the Tellings to his benefit. My brother trains new wizards in a gruelling fashion. Some cannot withstand the Trials and quit. He then gets them to agree to bar themselves from their magic forever. I understand the need to train magic wielders properly, but his approach is too severe."

"What happens if they use magic again after they leave?" Chip asked.

The wizard's face grew dark. "They cannot."

The boy looked at him funny. "But what if they do?"

"I think you misunderstand what I am saying. They cannot. He blocks them permanently."

Chip looked at him in shock. "How is that possible?"

The wizard sighed. "It is one of the reasons I left. If a student failed the Trials, they were barred from the Power. He spent a thousand years studying the Wall in a magic wielder's mind. He figured if the Unnamed One could find a way to remove it permanently, there must also be a way to make it unbreakable. In the end, he succeeded. It was surprisingly simple."

"How?" Chip asked in disgust.

"If a magic wielder fills themselves with every ounce of their Power and redirects it into rebuilding their Wall, they cannot break through again. Nobody had ever tried such a thing before. It seemed counterintuitive. The Wall gets removed in your mind to access the Power, but once it goes back up, your access stops. However, if you take all your Power at once and channel it into the Wall from this side, it becomes impregnable. The strength of the Wall then equals your Power, so it holds it back. You cannot break through again. It becomes a Permanent Wall."

"Who would ever agree to such a thing?" the boy asked in shock.

"Nobody, but eventually we all break. Anyone who refused to create a Permanent Wall became a prisoner in the fortress until they agreed. The longest someone held out for is one hundred and twenty-three years." Both Chip and the princess stared at him in disbelief.

"That's monstrous," the princess managed.

"That's Balor," the wizard said.

"Wait, can a Higher Level wizard break through someone's Permanent Wall?" Chip asked.

Xander shook his head. "No, the Wall is Permanent, a perfect seal, apparently unbreakable. They are forever shut out."

"That is plain wrong," the boy said. "Why do we have to go there anyway?"

"Balor commands and trains all the magic wielders of humanity. They swear fealty to him even above their monarch. Anyone Certified as a wizard in the Guild is loyal to him. He demands it. This was agreed upon by the High Kings of Amrika three millennia ago. However you view it, we need the wizards to build an army."

"That makes him the most powerful person in Amrika," Chase whistled. "Even above High King Dominor." He looked at his best friend. "Well, that makes you third, Guardian. That's not so bad."

"I have a feeling third is still the same as last with Balor," Chip replied sourly.

"Very astute, young man," Xander laughed. "You know him already!" The old man got up and stretched. "Let us be off, shall we? The Ancient Woods await. I think you will like them."

The companions continued following the path east.

2

The raven circled high overhead, watching them leave. Hate filled its eyes. Murk had stumbled back towards Thundar after the cornfield attack. His wound was serious and needed attention. He shapeshifted into the form of a young woman and knocked on the door of a farmer's home. The owner and his wife told him of a magic wielder in Thundar who could heal him. Murk let them dress his wounds as best they could then killed the farmers quickly before stealing a horse. He had no time to make the experience more enjoyable.

The Dark Elf arrived at the healer's house in Thundar late in the evening. The magic wielder was an old man at the Yellow Level with passable healing abilities. It was enough to mend his stomach wall and seal the wound, but it left a nasty scar. As soon as he finished, Murk turned into his true self and lashed out at the man for his incompetence. He decided to take more time with this one, honing his craft, which had lain dormant for far too long. Humans were frailer than Elves and required more patience.

Murk had an idealistic view of justice and felt the man's claims to be a healer were exaggerated, needing immediate rectification. Hopefully, by carrying out justice, others would be more cautious in their assertions. It was one of the ways the Dark Elf felt he contributed back to the world.

When he finished a long time later, Murk wiped the blood off the corner of his lips and gently reprimanded himself for being a bit overzealous. He would have preferred to carry on a little longer, but the healer's heart gave out. The Dark Elf reminded himself of the need for proper pacing. He was out of practice, after all. Murk sighed, vowing to do better next time. He decided to sleep until morning, as he would have difficulty tracking them at night. Besides, he was exhausted.

The Dark Elf awoke after sunrise and walked across the street to the general store in the guise of one of the dead soldiers from the cornfields. The owner looked at him funny when he gave the man a small plain nugget of gold for food, but he did not ask questions. Murk sat out back next to a fisherman's cabin to eat, watching a family prepare for the day. He talked to the young boat cleaner for a while, gleaning important information. He determined humans had changed somewhat over the millennia. They seemed even weaker. What a pathetic race.

When he finished eating, the shapeshifter shook hands with the cleaner to appear polite then walked to the outskirts of town. He flew away in raven form, leaving Thundar behind. Murk squawked as the pain in his side returned, reminding him that the healer did deserve the long lesson. At least he was able to fly.

Now, circling high above, he could see the boy wizard and his companions heading towards a huge forest. They were nearing the Guild, which meant he was running out of time. He especially wanted the girl. She meant so much to the boy that it would be plain wrong to leave her alive.

Her death would likely send the lad into endless fits of rage, even turning him into an asset for his Master. Ideally, Murk would have liked to pick them off one by one until only the Orb Stealer and the red-eyed boy remained.

He had to be wary though of this so-called Guardian's Power. He felt it as the boy razed the cornfields in rage after his pet dog died.

Murk had to admit he was incredibly powerful. The Dark Elf laughed at the thought of anyone caring for a wild beast, let alone feeling loss at its death. Humans were so odd.

He reviewed his options. All the guards were dead except one. He now wished he had targeted the others first. In fairness, he did not find out their destination until it was too late. Even the guards thought they were traveling to Toron where he could have easily killed them. The Guild was another matter, requiring a higher level of expertise. It was not beyond him, as he was the assassin master, but it came unexpectedly. His goal was to attack the girl before they reached the forest. Murk would assume the wasp form and end her life before the others could react. They would not expect an aerial attack.

After that, he would need to assume a different form more suitable for the woods. The Dark Elf needed to bring the boy in alive, which required careful execution. For now, he would focus on eliminating the girl and the two Protectors.

Murk moved far out of sight, changing into the demon wasp form. It was less elegant to fly than the raven but immensely powerful.

He stayed low, circling patiently, waiting for the princess to leave the group to relieve herself. He would then decapitate her and disappear. He smiled at the thought of the others searching for her only to find a headless body.

His chance did not materialize, however, sending him into a rage. Then, when it looked like they would all reach the safety of the forest, the young Protector stayed for a few moments in a thicket of trees. He was looking at something on the ground. Under cover of the same trees, the wasp demon dove straight down.

The Protector had no clue he was about to die but uncannily looked up at the last instant, somehow hearing or sensing the Dark Elf. Regardless, the wasp demon slammed into the pathetic human's chest and then gored the tall boy's stomach with his hind feet as he fell on his back.

Somehow, the young man pulled his sword out and struck back at the shapeshifter, knocking him sideways. Incredibly, the Protector stood up with his shirt in shreds, yet the boy's skin was only scratched. Murk recoiled, realizing something was not right.

Few things instilled fear in the Inner Circle member besides his Master, but this was one. As the boy advanced, Murk noticed red flecks in his eyes. He was not like other humans. The young Protector had changed.

The Dark Elf heard the others running up behind the trees, alerted to the commotion. Murk leapt into the air and flew like an arrow across the horizon. He felt a crackle of magic behind him and veered left, narrowly avoiding a red ball of fire. He dove from view behind the next hill, safe from attack. He continued flying a ways then resumed his raven form, which required much less energy.

He realized that his strategy needed a complete review. The companions to this boy were much more powerful than he had anticipated. Somehow, the Protector had changed. Murk landed in a valley and began walking in his natural form, mind already working on the problem. He was used to challenges. No great accomplishments were ever easy.

In a way he had not felt in a long time, the master assassin felt an excitement build in him. The beginnings of a plan emerged. He stood stock still, running the different scenarios in his mind. One plan stood out above the others. It was extremely bold but had a good probability of success if executed properly. It would take longer than he wished, but the results would be exhilarating. The Dark Elf began to laugh in his natural, high-pitched tone. His Master would be so proud of him. Murk leapt back into the air, shapeshifting into the raven, and soared eastward.

THEY ALL STOOD LOOKING at Chase. His shirt was torn to shreds, but his body was only mildly cut. Even as they watched, the wounds faded, healing themselves. He looked down, laughing in disbelief.

"It was the demon wasp. I sensed it a moment before it attacked, thinking it was a bird. The impact was crazy, but I barely felt it. After I stood up, its black demon eyes actually looked afraid. Then it heard you coming and took off." He stopped talking as they continued staring at him. Garth had one eyebrow raised.

"I almost got the wasp with a fireball, but it veered away and dove out of sight," Chip said in frustration. "I hope it comes back."

"Right," Xander said, still giving Chase a strange look. "I suggest we get to the safety of the forest. We are almost there. Keep alert until we are under the trees." They turned and followed the old man, glancing up in the sky, wary of another attack. Chase kept smiling, rubbing his stomach. Chip could not help but laugh. The boys rounded the next hill then stopped in disbelief.

Ahead of them was a forest with immense, towering trees. The path ran straight through an entrance bordered by two enormous stone statues, possibly of the same wizard. One showed a man with a sword facing an unseen enemy. The other had both hands raised, ready to unleash magic. A road went north and south along the forest's western edge, meeting the path. "Who are they?" Chase asked, looking in wonder at the statues.

"Oh, they are both my brother, Balor," Xander said indifferently. He pointed at the road bisecting the path. "This road leads south to Toron and north for many leagues, eventually reaching the Troll Kingdom. It is called the Frontier Road. The soldiers from the capital take this route to reach the front lines to defend against troll skirmishes."

The late afternoon sun shone behind them as they walked forward, illuminating the opening to the Ancient Forest. "It's beautiful," Chip breathed.

"My goodness, wait until you see the rest." The wizard winked.

Captain Melvin cleared his throat, and they all turned.

"This is the end of the road for me, I'm afraid. I will be heading back to Banfar." The others began to protest. "No, I need to return. I never told you, but I have a woman who is pregnant with child. I cannot stay here. Escorting you has been an honour, but my mission is complete. I wanted to make sure you reached the safety of the forest. I have much more to do in Banfar." Xander and Garth looked at the man and extended their hands, which he grasped.

"Thank you. Take this. It will get you back and then some," the wizard instructed, giving the captain the rest of his coin pouch. Melvin's eyes widened at the weight. "Take one supply horse. You have fought bravely. We will meet again in the Last Battle, the Creator willing. May you find good fortune in your travels." The others echoed the sentiment as the man wiped his eyes.

"It has been the greatest honour of my life." He saluted, and with a final wave, Captain Melvin took his leave.

The companions watched him round the hill, then turned to walk between the giant statues, which were easily one hundred feet high. The soft darkness of the forest enveloped them. The path continued through the giant trees, weaving between the trunks. The ground consisted of soft brown earth, like a carpet.

Smells of rich, mature wood permeated the air, interwoven with scents of flowers and damp forest floor. It was enchanting. Chip breathed deeply, remembering the mountains. He felt at home with nature. A great stress flowed out of him, and he smiled.

"Halt! Who breaks the ward to our home?" The voice came from somewhere ahead of them. The party stopped, listening.

The wizard stepped forward. "I do. I am Grand Wizard Xandrostika, brother to High Wizard Balor of the Guild, accompanied by the Guardian of Humanity, the Honorary High Commander of Toron, the Invincible Protector, and the Princess of Vanalon. We seek refuge."

Chase looked at Chip, mouthing, "Invincible Protector," all proud of himself. The princess rolled her eyes.

"Those are powerful titles. Why should we believe you?" called the voice.

"I think they are lying," chimed in a second voice. It seemed like both were coming from behind the tree in front of them.

"Thomas and Kristan, get out from behind there before I wring your necks," Xander said sternly. Almost immediately, two young, tall, handsome blond wizards popped out, followed by a much shorter black-haired one. They tried to keep a serious face but broke out laughing.

Xander could no longer contain his mirth and walked forward, clasping their hands and slapping them on the shoulders. "Ah, Jordy," he said, looking down at the diminutive wizard in brown robes with rich, dark skin. "It is good to see you. I assume you have passed the Trials."

Jordy nodded proudly. He had a square, good-looking face. "I passed two years after you left." He leaned in, whispering conspiratorially, "Things changed after you departed. Balor became even stricter, failing many students who would have been good wizards."

Xander sighed. "It is what I feared. I hope our news will change his views on the Trials. We need all the magic wielders we can find. A great battle is coming."

Thomas and Kristan looked at each other at the same time. They both wore long blue robes. "We are ready to fight," Kristan said, puffing out his chest. "It has been so boring since you left. Balor put us on a gruelling schedule mentoring everyone else since we are Blues. We have almost no time to get in trouble."

"My goodness, there's still plenty of time for that. How did you get here so quickly after we tripped the wards? Were you waiting for us?" the old wizard asked.

Kristan tried to answer again, but Thomas ribbed him. "We've been waiting here for three days. Balor had us stationed at the entrance, saying you would arrive shortly from Banfar. The High Wizard said you usually brought trouble, so he sent us Blues just in case." He looked down at the brown-robed wizard. "Jordy followed us. He was supposed to be patrolling the perimeter, but when he heard it was you, he insisted on joining."

Jordy tried to stand taller. "I am a powerful Brown and can be quite handy in a fight." He raised his chin and stood on his tiptoes, trying not to laugh.

Chase looked at them all, perplexed. "How old are you?" he asked the two blondes. Kristan covered Thomas's mouth before he could speak and answered.

"We were eighteen summers when we broke through our Walls. That was twenty summers ago." Seeing Chase's mouth drop, they continued, "Wizards age slowly once their Wall is broken, especially at the Higher Levels. We still look close to eighteen summers old even though we are thirty-eight."

They nodded as if it were obvious.

"I'm thirty-three," said Jordy. "I broke through seventeen summers ago when I was sixteen." He looked at Chip. "You must be the Guardian, whatever that means. How old are you?"

"Um, I'm sixteen summers. I broke through my Wall about a month ago," he said honestly. They all looked at him to see if he was joking.

"Oh, so you are new. That's fine. You have up to five years to finish the Trials. What Level are you?" asked Thomas.

"Uh... Red," Chip said, glancing at Xander. The wizard was trying not to laugh.

"Very funny. It's alright if you are Yellow or even Green. Most people are. There is nothing to be ashamed about. Kristan and I are very rare in the Guild. There are few Blues, and none of them are twins. Fraternal, to be clear." Thomas looked at his brother, who nodded sympathetically at the boy.

Chip stared at them, unsure if they were serious. They looked at him and waited. Finally, Kristan waved it off. "It is not important now." He put his arm around the boy's shoulders, consoling him. "We will find out soon enough. It's nothing to be embarrassed about. Our mission is to escort Grand Wizard Xandrostika and anyone accompanying him to the Guild. You are all guests of honour. Come, we have lots to show you." Chase was trying not to laugh. Eleanor elbowed him and put a finger to her lips.

"I agree," Xander chimed in. "No need to display bravado and compare Levels. We all fight for the same cause. Why don't you young men give our new recruits here the grand tour?"

"Our pleasure," said Kristan, bowing with a flourish. Thomas tried to step in front of him, but he knocked his twin out of the way. "Follow me."

"Excuse me!" a female voice sounded far behind them. They all turned to see a small, pretty girl with long dark hair standing on the road, looking flustered. "Is this the way to the Guild?"

She had a backpack on that was too large for her.

"State your business," Jordy called, pretending to be in charge.

"I am answering the call to be trained. I come from a village near Toron. My name is Mina." She had olive skin and looked to be in her late teens.

Jordy looked at Kristan, who shrugged. "New recruits do not get an escort, but since we are going this way anyway...it is up to you, Grand Wizard."

Xander also shrugged, looking her way. "The more the merrier. As I said, we all fight for the same cause." He waved the girl forward. "Wait, there's another coming." In the distance, they could see an overweight teenage boy with brown hair walking towards the forest on the same path they used. He rushed up to them, breathless, cheeks red.

"Hi, I'm Siz from Thundar. I heard about the call for training and wish to become a wizard. I have magic," he said proudly, lifting both pudgy hands as if to cast a spell on them.

Jordy rolled his eyes. "This is why I do not like doing forest patrol. Since the announcement to train new wizards went out a few weeks ago, we have seen a steady stream of recruits from all across Amrika. The monarchs have been ordered to send any magic wielders to the Guild at once to be trained for the upcoming Last Battle." He looked at Xander. "Are things really as serious as they say?"

"More than you know. A grave threat looms on the horizon. We must prepare. All are welcome. Come along, Mina and Siz. Join us for the tour." The rest of the group introduced themselves to the two newcomers, and everyone set off.

The twins led the way, heading eastward through the Ancient Forest. Chip was in awe of the monstrous three-thousand-year-old trees, which Xander said came from tiny seedlings in Fang Forest. The path weaved around some that were over forty feet around. Beautiful multi-coloured butterflies flitted above them, dancing through the slanting beams of the late afternoon sun. As the path meandered, Chip noticed a group of beautiful, sleek-coated reindeer chewing the leaves of a bright green bush. The animals stopped and gazed at the travellers with glistening brown eyes, unmoving. Some had antlers over six feet long.

Thomas pointed at the beautiful animals.

"All the wildlife was handpicked from across the lands to complement the forest. If you are lucky, we will catch a glimpse of the unicorns. They are all white, but recently a novice on forest patrol spotted a red one. I don't believe her, to be honest. The wards surrounding the woods keep all the animals in. According to the histories, the Great Forget caused a wide variety of unusual creatures, both good and bad. High Wizard Balor has amassed a collection of good ones over the millennia. But understand these are still wild animals and can be unpredictable. For instance, the Cuddly Bears will never harm you unless you try to cuddle them." He noticed Siz's open-mouthed expression. "I know. I don't get it either."

They continued walking, noticing odd animals they had never seen before. The whole place had an enchanted feel to Chip, and he was having trouble trying not to smile. A multi-coloured striped bird with a long feathered tail squawked at them from the lower branches of a large tree up ahead. Its beak was bright yellow.

Jordy waved at the creature. "Hey, Chirps, where have you been?"

The bird looked at him, turning its head. "Jordy. Little man. Nice day." It spoke in short, high-pitched quips." Chase laughed aloud, slapping his thigh.

Siz giggled, his large cheeks quivering. "What else can it say?"

Jordy shrugged. "It can copy almost anything. Give it a try."

"Hi, Chirps. Can you say, 'Hi, Siz. You are a powerful wizard.'"

The bird looked down at him, turning its head at an angle. "Hi Siz. Powerful. Fat. Wizard."

Jordy laughed and then noticed Siz turning red. "Chirps likes to insult people. He gets a kick out of it. Don't take him seriously."

Siz shrugged. "It's alright. Everyone used to make fun of me at school, but they all got scared when I broke through my Wall."

"When was that?" asked Kristan.

"A year ago. I did not want to come to the Guild at all because I was afraid of getting bullied again. I dropped out of school last year for that reason. Three weeks ago, the magistrate in Thundar sent soldiers house to house, ordering anyone with magic-wielding abilities to travel here for training. My parents told me I had no choice, so I left two days ago. You won't believe what I saw on the way up here." Siz shuddered.

"What did you see?" asked Thomas. Xander shared a look with Garth.

Siz looked around, whispering conspiratorially. "There was a great battle in the cornfields a day's walk west. Parts of these weird creatures were everywhere. I have never seen anything like them around Lake Supper. I must have just missed the fight. They are lucky because I could have done some serious damage." He puffed his chest out, which only jiggled his belly. "Someone with magic must have set fire to the rest of the cornfields because they were all burnt to the ground. Even I thought it was pretty impressive." They all looked at him. He waited, as if expecting some sort of praise. When none was forthcoming, he shrugged it off. "Anyways, they were lucky I arrived late."

"My goodness, quite interesting, lad," Xander said, nodding in understanding. "Those demons were lucky you were late. We did, however, manage to take care of them ourselves."

Siz's eyes widened. "That was you?"

The wizard nodded. The boy gulped and said nothing.

"Tales for another time though," Xander said with a smile. "Let's carry on."

They continued walking into the early evening as night fell. Chip stared in amazement as the moss surrounding the base of every tree lit up to provide a soft green light. More incredible still, glowing butterflies of every colour appeared above them, providing enough light to illuminate the canopy.

"It's magnificent," Eleanor breathed, looking around in wonder.

Thomas nodded. "Someone could walk all night if they desired.

Up ahead is a resting station. I suggest we eat dinner and then retire for the night. You must all be tired."

"And starved," Chase said to no one in particular.

They walked a short while longer before reaching a wide clearing with picnic tables surrounding a gazebo. A large fire pit sat off to the side with sitting logs, and a dozen empty hammocks were tied between the surrounding trees. Each hammock had a small tarp secured above it in case it rained. The clearing was full of butterflies, providing ample lighting.

"This is great!" squealed Siz, leaping onto a hammock that sagged considerably. The tour guides prepared the fire and rummaged through their packs for food. Garth and Chase laid out supplies on the table, and soon various meats were sizzling on the metal grill. Chip sat with Eleanor on a log surrounding the fire. Mina wandered over, looking shy.

The princess made room for her. "Come, sit. Do not be shy. So you are from Toron?"

"Yes," Mina replied. "Well, there's a small village a short ride north called... Quiver." She laughed nervously. "Almost nobody has heard of it."

Eleanor turned her head to think. "No, I have not. My mother made me go through all the villages and towns of Amrika over and over as a child, but I cannot recall that name." She looked puzzled. "Is it near Stonewood?"

Mina seemed unsure then nodded. "Yes." She looked around. "This place is beautiful. I never expected it."

The princess smiled. "Neither did I. You hear stories, but some sounded too farfetched for belief. Wizards do not usually talk about the Guild. In fact, most of them keep their magic-wielding abilities a secret."

"I can understand why," Mina responded. "People are a superstitious lot. It is better they do not know. I only came here because it is now required. Guards from the capital passed through a few days ago, saying anyone uncertified must be trained. I wanted to hide in my village, but my parents insisted."

She looked down. It was obvious how nervous she was.

"They allowed you to come by yourself?" Chip asked.

She looked at him quickly. "I do not need protection. I have had my Power for a long time. The village boys know not to trifle with me. Besides, it's only a day's walk."

"Come and eat, everyone," Jordy said, glancing at Mina and waving them over. They all had their fill of delicious, spiced lamb and beef with sides. As they were eating, the princess noted a family of small bears behind Siz.

"Oh my goodness, what cute bears!" Eleanor said in delight. It was a family of five with two plush-looking bears guiding three adorable tiny, furry cubs.

The twins turned as one. "Those are Cuddly Bears. They are generally harmless. Whatever you do, do not touch or feed them."

Even as he said it, Siz held out a steak for the father bear.

"No!" screeched the twins as one. The round, harmless-looking father bear suddenly bared ferocious fangs and snapped outwards, taking the pudgy boy's hand clean off. It was so fast that no one had time to move. Siz held up his wrist stump and screamed in terror. The bears, looking horrified, started making crying noises then turned and ran away. The twins rushed up to Siz and grabbed his shoulder, eyes blazing blue, sending healing energy into his arm, slowly calming him down. Another hand started to grow out of the stump.

"You aren't doing it right," said Kristan. "Give me the link."

Thomas rolled his eyes. "Fine, but you're no better." They kept arguing, but finally, a small hand evolved and grew to full size. They released their magic and exhaled. Both had a light sheen of sweat on their foreheads.

"Whew, that takes a lot out of you," Kristan explained. "It's much harder to regrow an appendage than fix a damaged one. Your hand will feel weak for a while, and the skin colour will be off, but it should adjust in no time. Please do not feed the Cuddly Bears. Trust me, we get it. The name should be changed. The problem is they are too damn cute to call them anything else."

Siz took it all in with wide eyes, still shocked at the whole ordeal. He looked at his new hand as if it was not his.

Xander smiled, shaking his head, then yawned. "Let's take watches tonight. I will take the first. Garth?" The weapons master nodded.

"Wake me in two hours."

"There is no need for a watch, Grand Wizard. The wards protect us. The Ancient Forest is safe," Thomas said respectfully.

Xander looked over at the blond young man. "Times have changed, lad. Until we reach the Guild, we must be vigilant."

Thomas nodded. "As you wish, Xandrostika. However, you have travelled far. I insist that my two companions and I take the first three watches. Please rest, and we will wake you when it is time."

The wizard was about to protest then yawned and agreed.

"Very kind. Thank you."

They each found a hammock spread throughout the clearing. Chip took one as close to the princess as possible. He did not want to leave her alone even though the place seemed safer than anywhere they had been so far.

She smiled at his concern, then waved him over. He leaned into her hammock to ask her what she needed. Before he could say anything, she grabbed the front of his shirt and pulled him down for a long kiss.

He struggled to get out, trying not to laugh. When the boy finally disengaged, he turned to see the twins giggling at him, giving him a thumbs up. He waved awkwardly and then crawled into his own hammock, amazed at how comfortable it was. He had heard of such a bed but never experienced one. It felt like a warm cocoon surrounding his body. The crackling of the fire further soothed him. Chip gazed at the beautiful luminescent butterflies flying amongst the treetops, and a feeling of comfort cradled him into a deep sleep.

3

They awoke to screaming as the sun broke the horizon. Chip sat up straight, about to reach for his Power. The sounds came from Siz, who was lying in his hammock, unable to move because a small creature was sitting on his chest. The twins were laughing. Jordy, who was on watch, tried to calm the screaming boy.

"It's just a wood sprite!" he yelled to Siz. "They come out in the mornings. All he wants is a berry."

"I...I...I don't have a berry," the boy quailed, looking on the verge of tears. The sprite, no taller than a foot, dressed in green woodsman clothes, stuck out a tiny tongue from his wizened face. He leapt off Siz and scurried off into the woods.

"See, that's all you had to say," Jordy said as if it was obvious. Siz glowered at him. The twins tried to stop laughing.

"Why did you not wake me?" Xander asked, giving the twins a reproachful look.

"No need. Besides, a Grand Wizard should not have to take watch," Kristan pointed out. Xander grumbled then nodded in gratitude.

"All right. Let's eat a quick breakfast, then off we go." The twins bustled about pulling out various supplies and, in short order, prepared a hearty meal of bacon and eggs.

"This is so good," Chase said between steaming mouthfuls.

Thomas laughed. "Wait until you reach the Guild. This is nothing." He did not elaborate. Chase nodded, continuing to chew happily.

The companions cleaned up and began following the path again. Chip felt a cool breeze and saw how much the leaves had already changed in the trees. Winter was on its way. Eleanor held his hand as they walked with Mina on her left. The small girl seemed to feel more comfortable around the princess. Siz decided to walk to their right. He seemed to talk a lot about the most mundane things. Chip did not mind as he frankly missed other forms of companionship.

They had travelled as such a tight-knit group for so long that he welcomed new personalities. He suspected there would be many more when he reached the Guild. The place was starting to sound like a combination of school and training. He was used to that.

The twins, leading the way, suddenly stopped. They both put a finger to their lips. Everyone halted, looking ahead. Then they heard it. The noise was soft at first then increased in volume. It was the rumble of horse's hooves, followed by a musical whinnying.

The sound got louder until a small herd of unicorns appeared ahead of them between the trees, shiny coats glowing in the morning light. All were white, surrounding one beautiful red stallion. Their smooth, polished horns were the colour of dark wood, except for the stallion. His was bright white.

Chip immediately felt a pull towards the beautiful animals, especially the red one. He had never seen such pure elegance embodied in a living being. He suddenly felt a hum at his waist and realized it was the dragon egg. Tucked away in her pouch, she was vibrating.

The red unicorn stopped and turned to face the boy. The other white ones slowed, spread out and halted, forming a circle around the group. The twins stood open-mouthed. The beautiful red creature walked up to Chip. He had bright, intelligent brown eyes and rippling muscles. The unicorn lowered his great head to the boy, the tip of his horn pointing at his feet.

Kristan stepped forward with a look of awe. "I think he wants you to ride him." The blond twin's voice trembled. "This has never happened before."

Chip felt the buzzing at his side grow more pronounced as if urging him forward. Incredibly, the noble creature took a knee, allowing the boy to leap onto his back. He did not know why, but it felt right. Chip sunk in between the unicorn's muscles, the grooves perfectly aligning with his body. He had no reigns, so he grasped the beautiful red mane. Tugging to the right, the horse adjusted instantly, turning in a circle. The other unicorns did the same, kneeling beside his startled companions.

The twins looked at each other in amazement, then leapt onto their white unicorns, letting out whooping laughs. Jordy had trouble scrambling up due to his height but finally managed to climb on. Garth leapt onto his mount without effort, then grabbed the reigns of the packhorse so it could follow. They looked at each other in disbelief. All the white unicorns turned to face the red stallion.

Thomas looked at Chip. "They are all waiting on you."

"On me? Well then, let's go for a ride!" The boy nudged the stallion in the ribs, and the unicorn sprang forward like a lightning bolt. The way he sunk into the horse's back made staying on easy. The unicorn was incredibly fast and fluid, running effortlessly down the meandering path. The wind caught Chip's hair, bringing with it the smells of the forest and life itself. The egg at his waist went silent as if her only purpose was to introduce them. He looked behind to see the others keeping pace. Everyone was smiling except Mina and Siz, who seemed fearful, hanging on for dear life. He laughed, flashed everyone a grin, and tapped his horse once more, leaning forward.

If Chip had thought he was going fast before, it would have been nothing compared to the speed he experienced next. For a moment, he imagined himself riding a red arrow shot from the most powerful bow in the world. A wildness gripped him, like running haphazardly through a field as a young boy or leaping off a waterfall for the first time. He hugged the unicorn's neck, becoming one with it.

The scenery blurred into colours, smells, and sounds. He ran with the horse, feeling the animal's wild spirit. The beast was free and proud, entering the prime of his life, facing things with reckless abandon, full of vitality and energy. They both felt invincible.

After a while, Chip looked back, hoping the rest of them shared the same joy. With a start, the boy realized he was alone. The others were nowhere in sight. He pulled up on the unicorn's mane, and the stallion slowed to a trot, still dancing nimbly. He realized it must be the first time anyone had ever ridden him. The boy did not know how he knew, but he just did. After a while, Chip heard the others before seeing them. They were galloping at an incredible speed, faster than any horse he had ever seen. The white unicorns reigned up on their own, slowing to a perfect stop in front of the stallion.

"Where were you?" he called to them. "Did you stop somewhere?"

They all looked at him funny. "Are you joking?" Chase asked. "We rode our fastest to keep up with you. Nobody slowed at all. You...were like a red blur. I've never seen anything move that fast." Everyone nodded.

"The histories say unicorns have magic," Kristan said. "It manifests in their speed. They talk of an elf who rode one once."

Thomas glared at him. "We don't talk about that elf, remember."

Xander looked amused. "It seems this red unicorn suits you. Perhaps you should give him a name."

Chip did not need to think. "Redmane."

The wizard nodded. "Once our packhorse arrives, you can lead the way. I recommend you slow the pace a bit for the poor thing to keep up." Chip realized that Garth was not holding the supply horse's reigns anymore. The weapons master shrugged, making the boy grin. He knew Garth could not resist feeling the speed of a unicorn either.

"I still cannot believe we are riding them!" Thomas exclaimed to Kristan. They both let out a whoop of laughter. "Wait until the others hear about this!"

"At this pace, we should reach the Guild by early afternoon," Xander said, quite pleased. "Keep a steady trot, and we will be fine."

They waited until the packhorse finally galloped up, snorting angrily. The unicorns seemed to look away in snobby disdain. Garth grabbed the reigns with his left hand while his mount turned to the right, refusing to acknowledge the lowly pack animal. Chase laughed.

The group continued, letting the wonders of the Ancient Forest surprise them. They passed two more rest stations, the second filled with animals. Squirrels, rabbits, and foxes sat in a circle surrounding a giant owl. The bird gazed solemnly at the procession of unicorns, large yellow eyes unblinking. The other animals seemed irritated at the interruption, as if the owl was lecturing them. Nobody said a word as they passed through.

Jordy looked puzzled, staring at the twins, who seemed equally perplexed. "Was that what I think it was?" he asked. The twins shrugged, trying not to laugh.

They moved on, seeing several more wood sprites peeking at them from behind logs. Chip could not contain his curiosity any longer.

"What are they?" he asked.

Following his gaze, Thomas said, "Oh, them? They are harmless. Nobody can hear what the sprites are saying because they whisper. Once, an inquisitive wizard did a study on them and determined they were only spouting gibberish. They are expert tailors who use various forest materials to create clothes, and they like berries. That's all we know."

The blond wizard stopped talking, as if that was enough of an explanation. Chip waited for more, then looked at Eleanor, who was covering her mouth. He gave up and continued looking around, not wishing to miss anything.

Several flying squirrels flew at them from an overhanging branch, clearly angry they had imposed on their territory. The unicorns were not impressed with the antics and snapped as they came close, causing the flying pests to veer away at the last moment. It was enough, however, to produce a shriek from Siz, which appeased the furry rascals, who scurried away. Other wildlife made appearances, such as the armadillo families, oversized porcupines, and slow-moving anteaters.

At one point, they entered a clearing and saw a half-dozen large, orange creatures sitting in a circle. On closer inspection, they were big, overweight cats sitting on their haunches, faces looking skyward, large white bellies exposed. They started meowing when they sensed the travellers but refused to look at them.

"Ah, Chaircats, there you are," Kristan said. "I was wondering where you went." He pulled up his unicorn, and the others followed suit.

"What do they do?" Eleanor asked, intrigued.

"Nothing," Thomas answered. "They wait for someone to sit on them." The princess looked at him blankly. He rolled his eyes then leapt off his unicorn to demonstrate, plopping straight onto a Chaircat. Immediately, the animal began purring. Eleanor looked around for a moment then squealed and jumped down. She took a breath and sat back on the plumpest Chaircat. It started purring.

"It is soooo....soft and comfortable. I'm calling this one Tigger." She sank back on the animal and closed her eyes. Mina looked around, then climbed down from her unicorn and sat on an empty one. When it started purring, she giggled shyly. Everyone took a turn except Siz. Everything seemed to scare the boy. Then again, he did have his hand recently bitten off by a Cuddly Bear, so no one blamed him.

After the relaxing break, they continued onwards until the sun was high in the sky, and Chase began grumbling about lunch. Instead of stopping to eat, the twins waved them forward with a grin. Up ahead, the path approached a beautiful fountain along a much wider road that ran north.

A statue of a young wizard made of marble stood tall and proud in the center of the fountain. The water came out of his finger as if he was releasing magic. Once again, it looked like the young man was sculpted in the image of Balor. Xander glanced at Chip as he made the connection.

"He may have a bit of a complex," the wizard said sarcastically.

Three paths converged at the fountain from the east, south, and west. There was only one direction to go. They all turned north, following the finger of the pointing wizard. Ahead of them, the remaining trees thinned to reveal a wide bridge with a high arc. The forest ended at the bridge. They could not see anything beyond as the arc completely covered their view. The twins rode to the top of the bridge and waved them forward, trying to hide big smiles. Chip urged the unicorn to the peak and stopped at the top. The others joined him.

No words could describe what he saw.

Ahead of them, across a green, perfectly manicured lawn, was the Wizard's Guild. It was the largest castle he could have imagined. Instead of towers, four immense statues, two men and two women, stood at the corners of a gigantic rectangle with one arm raised, pointing skyward. Each wore different-coloured robes. High walls connected to the base of the towering statues. Across the tops of the crenellated walls, students and wizards walked. Some stopped and began pointing at them. The road led to a monstrous metal gate, which was closed.

More people began gathering at the top of the wall. Based on the layout, he inferred there must be a giant courtyard in the middle of the fortress. Below him, a river ran beneath the bridge, joining other rivers surrounding the castle.

"Quite a sight, is it not?" Thomas said, looking at their faces. "From all accounts, it is the largest building in Amrika. The statues go one thousand feet into the sky. You can actually climb to the top of each finger. The walls are two thousand feet long and two hundred feet high. The idea is if both statues at each end fell towards each other, their outstretched fingers would touch. The base of each statue holds the student dorms for each Level. Yellow and Green are at the back of the rectangle, and Blue and Brown are at the front. The suites for the Higher Levels are larger, as there are fewer students. We will find out soon enough which ones you fit into," he laughed.

Chip glanced at Xander, who looked amused. He wanted to ask

where a Red Level would go but realized how silly it would sound. Eleanor looked at him with some concern, realizing they would likely be separated. He would see about that. Chip noticed Jordy was looking at Mina. It was obvious the young man found her attractive. He was likely hoping she would be in his Level.

Kristan picked up where his brother left off. "The rivers that surround the Guild are warded with powerful magic. Some of the world's deadliest species of fish and reptiles are in these waters. Do not put your hand in." He turned and looked pointedly at Siz, who was scratching his belly, pretending he would never do such a thing. "The lawns in front of the castle have nests of dormant vipers that will trigger if the Guild is attacked."

"What triggers them?" asked Chase.

"It's obviously a secret," Kristan said, looking at him as if he was daft. "I know it is a word, but I am not sure which."

"What if someone says the word by accident?" Chase asked innocently.

Kristan squinted, trying to figure out if he was serious. "Obviously, it's a rare word."

"It is actually a phrase," Xander intervened, "and yes, I know it. I do hold some rank, after all."

"Of course, Grand Wizard. No one implied otherwise." Kristan tried to keep a straight face. "I suppose you do not wish to divulge the phrase. I would only use it if Jordy is crossing."

Jordy looked mollified. "Not nice." He sniffed, pretending to be offended.

"I see we have caused quite a stir," Xander remarked, pointing at the walls. A crowd of students had gathered on the top, pointing and waving. "We are likely the first visitors to ever arrive on unicorns. This will be quite the tale. Let us introduce ourselves, shall we?" The twins bowed their heads.

"Yes, Grand Wizard," they said in unison, leading the way.

The others followed, taking in the vast structure before them. They made it to the bottom of the bridge before the unicorns balked. Redmane would not set foot off the bridge onto the road leading to the gates. Chip noticed that the lawn started there as well. Perhaps the unicorns sensed the vipers, he thought. Or else this was as far from the Ancient Forest as they would go. He gently nudged the stallion's ribs one more time, but he would not budge. The others experienced the same problem. He sighed and dismounted, feeling a twinge of separation. The beautiful, red unicorn turned his graceful head towards the boy, nuzzling his cheek. Chip patted the big animal on the neck. The rest of them climbed down.

"I hope to ride with you again one day," he said to Redmane. In response, the unicorn shook his glorious coat and stood up on his hind legs, emitting a marvellous, musical neigh that carried to the Guild. The other unicorns followed suit, producing a stunning melody of sound. With that, they all turned and galloped back across the bridge to disappear into the Ancient Forest.

Everyone stared at each other, realizing they had witnessed something extraordinary. No words were necessary. They would only serve to downplay the moment.

The twins turned forward again, leading the way. Crossing the vast expanse of the lawn took longer than expected. From the walls, they must have looked like tiny figures far below. They arrived before the monstrous gates and stopped.

Xander glanced at them. "Balor keeps them closed for effect. He knew exactly when we crossed the ward. He likes to demonstrate his power at all times."

As they looked up, a figure with long white hair appeared in blue robes atop the gates. "Who goes there?" he bellowed. The walls were lined in either direction with students and teachers.

"That's Skylar, the old curmudgeon," Xander whispered to them. "He's worse than Balor in every way." He cleared his throat, calling back up formally, playing the game. "I am Grand Wizard Xandrostika, brother to High Wizard Balor, accompanied by the Guardian, also known as the Signal Fire Lighter, the Murderer of Demons, the Bane of the Inner Circle, the Destroyer of General Morgo, the Mountain Toppler, and the Slayer of the Black Dragon. I present to you the

Guardian of Humanity, Chip Oathbinder." He swept his hands towards the boy, pausing to catch his breath.

There was dead silence.

Then, startled murmurs and gasps ran through the crowd on the wall. Chip felt like every eye in the world was on him. Applause broke out slowly and grew in intensity. The twins and Jordy gaped at him. Mina stared downwards, and Siz's eyes were wide.

"He forgot 'the Burier of the Dim,'" Chase said absently.

"And?" The man in blue robes asked casually, seeming unimpressed.

Xander continued as if expecting the response. "I am also accompanied by the Weapons Master, the Champion of the Silver Sword, the Demon Slayer, The Trainer's Trainer, the High Commander of Vanalon, the Protector of the Grand Wizard, and the Honorary High Commander of Toron, Garth Stone." The weapons master said nothing, but Chip noticed him raise an eyebrow at "The Trainer's Trainer." The crowd responded with nods and loud applause, recognizing a legend of the Guild.

"And?" the voice above almost sounded bored.

The wizard continued, "I am also in the presence of Her Highness, the daughter of Queen Charlotte and the late King Barton, the sister to the late King Rupert, the Conjurer of Water, the Decapitator of Serpents, the Slayer of the Inner Circle, and the Burier of Demons. I present to you Princess Eleanor of Vanalon." He pointed at the girl, who turned in a circle and curtsied, used to such recognition. The crowd oohed and awed and broke out in applause.

"And?" There was a note of irritation in Skylar's voice.

"I am also accompanied by the Invincible Protector, Chase Longfellow." There was dead silence. People mouthed "invincible," not understanding.

Chase looked at the wizard in disbelief. "You could have at least said "Demon Slayer," he complained.

"Already used," the wizard said shortly. The awkward silence continued.

"And?"

Xander looked behind him. "We have two new students who joined us, excited to become wizards. Here are Mina and Siz. The crowd politely clapped. "The rest, you know." He waited.

The blue-robed wizard looked down. "Your titles are suitable enough to gain passage into the Guild. The two new recruits are to report to their alleged Levels immediately. They will be Assessed and verified tomorrow. The others are required in the council chambers immediately at the request of High Wizard Balor. He will meet you when he has time." Skylar looked around. "Any student, or teacher for that matter, not in class in the next ten count will be severely punished."

He turned around and strode off, counting down from ten. A mad dash of footsteps and bodies bumping into each other sounded atop the walls as everyone scrambled to class.

The giant gates opened at the same time. Skylar was now standing on the ground, waiting for them to enter. Chase looked at Chip, perplexed as to how the old wizard had made it down so fast. The boy shrugged. In the distance, Chip could make out an enormous courtyard in the center of the Guild, as he had surmised. Classes of students were either sitting on the grass listening to an instructor or practicing magic with a partner. Off to the side, he could make out Protectors, who were sparring with wooden swords.

"Greetings, Skylar," Xander said cordially, walking up.

"Its Grand Wizard Skylar, Xandrostika," the old man answered acidly.

"Then extend me the same courtesy, Skylar."

The man gave him a withering look, then turned to Mina and Siz. "Go with the greetor behind me in black robes. He will place you in your professed Level. You will see the Assessor tomorrow. Go now." He looked at the twins and Jordy, who immediately scurried away. To the others, he simply said, "Follow me."

They turned to their left and crossed the interlocking stone in front of the gates towards a giant set of wooden doors that led into the robes of the blue statue. The outer walls surrounding the huge courtyard were wide, like a rectangle with very thick borders. Similar doors on the opposite side of the gates led to the Brown Level statue. Chip could feel the crackle of magic everywhere. It became like a body buzz that made him tickle. The whole place exuded crazy energy, which he rather liked.

Skylar led them through the doors into a huge, wide hall. The boy felt the entire palace in Vanalon could fit into this one room. Xander hung back for a moment and whispered to him. "If he tries to enter your mind, resist it. Make it clear your memories are your own."

The boy nodded and thought of a question, but the wizard had moved up to confer with the weapons master. He busied himself by looking at the huge murals covering different sections of the walls. Battle scenes depicting wizards, elves, and demons were bright and vivid. The mural near the end of the hall showed the white barrier, which seemed to pulsate even in the picture. Off to the sides were large classrooms with wooden desks.

Polished gold doors stood closed at the end of the large hall. Skylar rested his hand on the right door, palm outward, and pulled the handle. It opened without a sound. He ushered them into a large anteroom with a further set of smaller shiny gold doors. An old man in green robes wearing glasses sat at a spotless desk.

"Good day, cleric," Skylar said formally. "Is the High Wizard here?"

The cleric nodded. "A moment, please, Grand Wizard Skylar." He stood up and walked across the rich, plush carpet to the door on the right, knocking once before slipping in. He re-emerged almost immediately. "You may enter. Wait until he acknowledges you."

The cleric held open the shiny gold door, and they walked through.

4

The Wizard's Guild council room was a cavernous hexagon with an immense oak table in the middle, forming the same shape. Every section had a colour painted on the wall behind it, signifying each Level. Sitting on a raised dais in the White Section was High Wizard Balor. He wore opulent blue robes with white embroidery around the cuffs. Behind him and to the side stood a man dressed all in black, bristling with weapons.

Balor did not look up when they entered but continued writing. They stood awkwardly for several moments. He finally leaned back, raising his eyes. Chip immediately noticed the resemblance to Xander. The High Wizard had long, flowing white hair surrounding a younger face than the boy expected. His strength in the Power for a Blue was considered unmatched in humans and likely caused him to age less than his younger brother. The man's strong features gave him a commanding presence, amplified by piercing, bright blue eyes.

"That was quite an entrance you made, brother," Balor said in a clear, strong voice. The monikers were... creative. Mountain Toppler? Bane of the Inner Circle? The Invincible Protector?" He noticed the cleric still standing in front of the door. "Leave us," he snapped, waving a hand. The cleric hastily bowed, then slipped out.

"Simply setting the stage," Xander replied smoothly.

"I would like you all to sit at the table where you feel you belong."

Balor leaned back, waiting. They glanced at each other and then sat at the side corresponding to their Level. Chase looked at Garth, who stood behind Xander in the Blue Section, then shrugged and moved behind Chip, who had pulled out the only chair in the Red Section. The princess sat further down in the Brown. Skylar moved to the Blue Section and sat as far over as he could from Xander.

When they were all seated, Balor looked around and nodded. His piercing eyes locked on the princess, who lifted her chin and returned his gaze. Chip knew Eleanor had experience in royal games and would not show weakness.

"Have you passed the Trials, Princess of Vanalon?"

"Trials?" she asked in an even voice.

"The Wizard Trials." He waited for her response.

"No, High Wizard. I just arrived, so I could not have passed the Trials."

"Then stand up. That seat is reserved for those who are Certified Brown Level wizards." His tone was unmistakable. She nodded imperceptibly, then stood up without changing her expression, though Chip noticed a slight tightening around her eyes. The princess pushed the chair in and stood behind it. Chip felt a stir of anger and stood up as well, pushing his chair in.

"What do you think you are doing?" Balor said sharply, turning to him.

"I have not passed the Trials either, so I am standing."

"Sit down!" he commanded in a strong voice. "I do not know what foolish titles my brother has bestowed upon you, but I am the High Wizard of Amrika. You do not get up unless I tell you." Chip studied the man, trying to remain calm.

Flashbacks of Miss Stern and King Barton appeared in his mind. A simmering rage began to brew. He had been through too much to be treated like this. He instinctively looked at Garth, who shook his head slightly. Chip immediately fell back on his training and wrapped himself in the Calm.

"As you wish," he said and sat back down.

"As you wish, High Wizard," Balor corrected him then waited.

Chip felt the Calm waver but remained steady. "As you wish, High Wizard."

"Good. Now, who are you?" Balor asked, looking at Chase as if he was an insect.

"I am Chip's Protector, High Wizard," he said as formally as he could.

"Really. Have you passed the challenges certifying you as a Protector for the Guild?" Balor asked.

"Well, no. I have been trained…"

"Get out!" Balor commanded.

Chase stopped talking, flustered. He looked around, backed up and bowed hurriedly before almost running out.

The High Wizard looked at Xander. "If he becomes a Protector and if this boy gets Certified, I will reconsider."

"How considerate, Brother," Xander said icily.

Balor ignored him and looked back at Chip. "Have you passed the Trials?"

"No, High Wizard," the boy said.

"Then stand up."

Chip maintained the Calm and rose, pushing in his chair.

"Good. Now everyone knows their place. I find conversations difficult when participants have assumptions about their positions." Balor paused, then looked at his brother. "You have been gone a long time, Xandrostika. It seems you have finally found a red-eyed magic wielder. Whether he is 'The One' is another matter entirely. I have ascertained many things through my network, but I would like to hear your version of events. Start from the beginning, and do not leave anything out."

Xander took a moment and began his story sixteen summers ago when he left the Guild. He recounted travelling through Thundar and meeting the Teller Zinduk on the way through. Chip had never heard this part and listened attentively. Xander recited the Seer's words verbatim. "Heed the queen's message. The boy is the One. He must suffer first to know love. Do not intercede until you must, and must you will. Then his training can begin." Chip's eyes widened. Skylar produced a sheaf of paper from the interior of his voluminous robes and scrawled the wizard's statements.

Xander continued, describing the orphan's upbringing and successful progression through training and school. Chip disliked Balor but conceded the High Wizard was able to listen.

Only when Xander reached the part describing Morgo's death did the High Wizard turn his head, glancing at the boy, his face unreadable. The wizard explained how Queen Charlotte insisted on staying behind to defend the city. This, of all things, caused Balor to make a strange expression. Chip thought it was regret but could not understand why. He looked at the princess, who shrugged. Skylar's face was devoid of emotion, but he did look down.

When the retelling reached the part with the Dim, the High Wizard's eyes narrowed, and Chip thought he could detect a glint of fear. Xander proceeded to describe Han's Telling verbatim as Skylar scribbled furiously.

The wizard recounted the retrieval of the white dragon egg and the harrowing escape from the Dim, ending with the toppling of Cave Mountain on the relentless creature. He stressed the word 'toppling,' evidently to back up his 'Mountain Toppler" moniker used earlier to describe the Guardian. The intonation did not escape Balor's notice, who pursed his lips. The female egg's request to 'Follow the son of Arkan to the Guild and build an army' was mentioned, which Skylar wrote down.

Xander continued with their trek to Banfar and the revelations from Silvermane's mind. Balor showed a rare glimpse of surprise that Elf King Luminor had been the one to deposit the orphan at the gates of Vanalon. The wizard described how he named Chip 'The Guardian", which the people took up, changing the very nature of Banfar from debauchery to hope. Skylar grudgingly nodded in approval. The expedition across the Great Plains elicited no response until they reached Thundar, where Zinduk pronounced her Telling, which Skylar recorded.

The wizard finished with the terrible battle in the cornfields whereby Silvermane perished, and the wasp demon escaped. He described Chip's healing of Chase and the princess, causing a transformation in both. The tall boy's newfound abilities justified the 'Invincible Protector' moniker. Out of everything Balor heard, this produced the biggest reaction. He looked sharply at his Protector behind him. Xander wrapped up his tale with their journey through the Ancient Forest on unicorns, then sat back and exhaled.

Balor's eyes blazed an incredible blue as a pitcher on a side table lifted by itself to pour a glass of water, which levitated to the table in front of Xander. The wizard thanked him and drank deeply. Chip was amazed at the dexterity of Balor's use of magic. "Quite a story, Brother. It gives me much to think about." The High Wizard stared at the boy. "I would hear your version, orphan. Better yet, I will see it through your mind."

A strong presence suddenly entered Chip's thoughts, searching. Instinctively, he wrapped it in the Calm, which revealed a range of Balor's memories. One seemed out of place, almost hidden, so he pulled it up as time slowed.

Arkan sat at the head of a table in a large tent, wearing blue robes with a pyramid embroidered on the front. Standing before him was Balor, barely an adult, trying to contain his rage.

"I am the rightful heir to the position of High Wizard," the young man almost shouted.

"You lack patience and control and are too impulsive, Son. Your brother is the better choice. Besides, the council will vote on who they deem best. Remember, we serve and defend the people of Amrika. Never forget that."

Balor stood in defiance, facing his father. "You favour Xandrostika because he stole the Orb. Is it fair that the council will vote him over me for that small achievement? Or worse, they will select King Jaggar. I refuse to have the council led by a....troll!" He nearly spat.

Arkan looked at his son, and his face softened.

"I have given you the Galad Prophecy to prepare you for the future. Tomorrow, we will push the demon horde back to the ocean and seal them off. I want you and Xandrostika to stand by my side while we finally subdue our enemy. This prophecy speaks of a sacrifice I must make before the Last Battle finishes. I think I know what it means. It is the oldest, most powerful Telling we have from Galador, the greatest Elf Seer. Few know of its existence. Keep it so. Galador told the Elf Kings that revealing it could taint other prophecies or make them self-fulfilling. This is why the kings kept it from magic wielders. It was meant for their ears alone. However, a separate, more recent Telling from the young Seer Skylar, whose predictions are gaining prominence, told King Luminor that times have changed, and it must be shared with me and my eldest son only. Skylar said you may tell others when it is time. You will know this when another finds out."

He sighed, displaying a great weariness, then looked at Balor. "I love you, Son. Your time will come. One day, you will acknowledge the one who will replace even you, and the circle will complete. We can spend our whole lives fighting prophecy or accept it. Remember, we serve the people."

Balor looked at him, the anger gone. His eyes were wet. "I love you too, Father."

Chip felt a sudden wrench as the High Wizard pulled sharply out of his mind and stood up angrily. "How dare you!" he yelled at the boy. Skylar rose with a shocked expression. Balor's eyes flared a brighter blue. The Protector standing behind the High Wizard widened his stance, putting a hand over the pommel of his sword. Garth turned slightly, at the ready.

The boy watched all this unfold, still shocked at the memory of Balor going against his father's wishes. His surprise mixed with anger after realizing Xander should have been next in line for High Wizard.

Balor reached for him with his substantial Power. Chip watched as if in slow motion, assessing the situation. This man might be the High Wizard of the Guild, the most powerful person in all of Amrika, but he was the Guardian. He served humanity. Flashes of all the people who mattered raced through his mind. Little Han and Beth, Auntie Clare, his companions, Rabbit, the citizens of Banfar, the young wizards in training, and all the other innocent humans living in Amrika.

They deserved the right to know the hidden prophecy. One man should not have that much power. Though the High Wizard ranked above him, he knew his duty was to protect the people.

He was Chip Oathbinder, and he would honour his duty.

The boy seized his Power, eyes blazing a ferocious red. The High Wizard tried to wrap him in blue magic, but he raised his hand and pushed it back. Skylar recoiled then added his blue Power to the High Wizards'. They both raised their hands, pointed at Chip and unleashed everything they had. The boy pulled deep of his reserves and held back their combined force. He surrounded himself with a crackling shield of pure red Power, electrifying the very air in the room.

Chip lifted both hands and pushed them away, then surrounded the pair with red magic. He realized his Power had grown since the last time he used it. Balor gasped, straining at the wall of red that enveloped him. His Protector pulled his sword out with a blur of speed, followed by Garth, responding in kind.

"No," Chip said, freezing both Protectors in place with his Power. The boy stood before them all, a shimmering torrent of red energy. Skylar's magic gave out, and he sank back, exhausted. Balor stood his ground, refusing to yield even though the boy could crush him if he chose.

Xander stood up, a look of amusement on his face. "Now, now. I think that will do. It was inevitable that the two of you should cross swords. As you said, Brother, it is important not to assume one's position. Now that we understand each other properly, let's get down to business."

Balor looked at Xander with gritted teeth then back at Chip, and dropped his hands. "Stand down," he said over his shoulder to his Protector. His blazing blue eyes returned to normal. He turned to stare at his brother. "You knew this would happen," he said accusingly. Chip withdrew his Power and re-established the Wall.

Xander smiled. "It was unavoidable. The boy is an apt student, but he will not be forced. If you tread on his sense of right and wrong, beware. His mind is his own, and enter it at your peril. The boy's abilities are different from ours. He has a mastery of the Calm, allowing him to glean important information from our memories. Chip is well-trained. He is the first to be versed in protection and magic wielding. Garth has instilled in him discipline and honour. The other boy, Chase, may be the greatest Protector ever born."

Balor sniffed, turning to his Protector, who had sheathed his sword. The man had a stern, square face framed by short black hair with grey at the temples.

"What do you think, Maxim? Do you think Chase can beat your greatest pupil, Carvor?"

Maxim turned his head and bowed to the High Wizard. "My pupil is undefeated and holds the Silver Sword. He will accept any challenge." Balor nodded, smiling.

Skylar looked at them all in disbelief, then turned to the High Wizard. "Are you going to allow this affront to go unchecked in the council room of all places? This boy has dared to raise a hand against you!"

Balor looked at him and then at the Guardian. "In fairness, I did seize my Power first. I needed to see his strength and whether he could control himself. Both of us learned the answers rather quickly."

"But, he is not even Certified. How dare he…" Skylar sputtered.

"Enough," Balor looked at the Grand Wizard. "Know your place, Seer." He turned to the boy. "You have great Power, Chip Oathbinder. I have waited for you for a very long time. You may have a seat at the table of the council."

Chip shook his head. "Not until she does," he said, indicating the princess.

A look of anger briefly crossed Balor's face, but it vanished just as fast. He turned to his brother. "Demanding, isn't he?"

"He believes in loyalty," Xander said with a look of approval. "A bit idealistic, perhaps, but were we not all?"

"Very well, I will grant you this courtesy. In normal times, I would never break such protocol, but these are the end times. The prophecies speak of it," Balor intoned. "You may both sit, but do not infer my lenience for weakness."

The princess nodded and pulled out her chair, sliding onto the soft, embroidered cushion. Chip did the same, then looked Balor square in the eyes.

"Will you tell us what you know of the prophecy?" he said without breaking his gaze, making sure the High Wizard understood he was referencing the memory just witnessed.

Balor sighed and nodded. "A long time ago," he began, "before the Breaking, there was an elf Seer named Galador." Skylar glared at the High Wizard, his features darkening. Xander watched him, eyes narrowing. "Galador was old but revered for his Tellings. Some say he never spoke a false prophecy. Before his mysterious death, he went up to the Elf Caves with a piece of parchment and remained there all night. By morning, he returned, insisting on seeing the Elf King, mumbling phrase upon phrase. None could rouse him from his trance-like state, and he refused to eat. His face grew gaunt, and his voice failed. They said his lips still moved in the end, though no sound came out, and then his heart stopped. The Elf Kings passed the parchment down secretly for generations until finally King Luminor gave it to our father, Arkan, before the Last Battle."

Xander's eyes widened. "I know of Galador, but only the Elf Kings were allowed to see his prophecies. Why have you not told me of this?"

"Skylar's prophecy forbade our father from disclosing it to anyone besides his eldest son until the day arrived when someone found out. That day has arrived," Balor explained. Xander looked doubtful, glancing at Skylar with distrust, then turned to study Chip, who nodded, verifying that it matched Balor's memory. "Skylar, retrieve the Galad Prophecy."

The old Seer gave Balor a venomous look and controlled himself. "This is not wise. The very knowledge of this prophecy can affect the Paths."

"That's the point. If not now, when? Surely when your Telling said not to disclose it all those years ago until someone found out, you were being truthful, old friend?"

Skylar scowled. "The Telling speaks through me. I am only the vessel. This boy is not ready."

Balor's eyes took on a dangerous glint. Chip could see why people feared this man. He repeated in a tone that few, if any, would challenge. "Retrieve the Galad Prophecy."

Skylar shrank back, then bowed low and pushed out his chair. He walked across the plush carpet to a painting, lifted it, then set it down. Behind it was nothing. Resting his hand on the wall, his eyes blazed blue, and he whispered something. A shimmering border appeared in the shape of a square with a handle.

He grasped it and turned, pulling on the small door, which opened smoothly. Skylar reached inside with both hands and carefully withdrew a piece of yellow parchment. Cradling it like a newborn babe, he walked over to the High Wizard and lightly rested it on the table before him. Xander leaned forward, eyes full of wonder. The Seer stood to the side.

"Behold, the Galad Prophecy," Balor intoned. "It is the oldest living prophecy and has never spoken false." He cleared his throat and began reading.

A Great Magic hath changed the world,
We have Forgotten who we were,
To become what we must,
The Elves will Break,
The Dark will rise,
Fear the red-eyed one,
For he will change the world,
His blood is from Before,
It links the Past,
The Orb will imprison the Dark Lord,
If the highest wizard makes sacrifice,
Yet strong will the Dark grow,
The Balance may break,
And all is lost,

Ware the Dim Darkness,
Nigh a mountain can hold,
Such a Touch as this,
Ends all things,
The Paths dwindle,
Two dragons collide,
If the wrong falls,
Woe be to life,
The white dragon links,
To a red-eyed Babe,
Left by a King,
Protected by the Wolf,
The Queen will die,
Soon after the Wolf,
He will seek vengeance,
Two paths remain,
His Rage may destroy all,
Or His Love can restore hope,
He will choose,
The Red Eye awaits,
Holding the Gift,
Three kings must bend,
Or all is lost,
The Dark will come,
And the Nothing,
Too strong for him,
She must wake,
Then sleep forever,
The Balance calls,
Through the Young Seer,
He holds the Key,
He is the Last Prophecy.

Balor stopped and looked around. Skylar continued scowling. Xander's brow furrowed. "This is similar to Skylar's Prophecy from three millennia ago with some important additions." He kept his voice level.

The High Wizard sighed again. "As I said, Skylar's Telling long ago forbade its full reveal to anyone but me. King Luminor and Arkan believed it was necessary to safeguard this parchment. Through Skylar's Core Prophecy, you knew much already. Our father's sacrifice is only mentioned in the Galad Prophecy, and your knowledge of it may have affected the outcome. At least that is what Grand Wizard Skylar believes."

Xander studied the Seer, who kept his face devoid of expression. Chip could tell that Xander knew something but his expression changed. "Very well. If that is what my father wished, I take no issue with it."

Chip still felt full of rage. "This prophecy is false. She is not a queen. I have already saved her life in the cornfields. She almost died." He looked around. "We are safe here. This does not make sense." His frustration showed. "Prophecies can be wrong. We have free will."

"This one has never been wrong," Balor stated, looking at the boy. "Does it not speak true? From the Breaking to the Orb imprisoning the Demon King through our father's sacrifice, King Luminor leaving you as a babe, the young Seer, linking with the dragon, the mountain falling on the Dim, and the wolf dying. Other prophecies have confirmed many parts."

Chip shook his head. "But I saved her... and she is not a queen."

Balor's face softened, "I am sorry, Eleanor. The Galad Prophecy even speaks true to your title. I am afraid I have grave news." She looked up at him in fear. Chip felt uneasy. The High Wizard sighed heavily, a rare look of sadness crossing his features, and looked into her eyes. "Vanalon has fallen. We received a message from your mother, Queen Charlotte, yesterday. The demons split the Calgar force in half during the retreat, cutting off escape. Your mother stayed behind to defend the city with Captain Peters to the last, killing many demons." He paused. The princess's eyes welled with tears. "She climbed to the top of the tower and released the last messenger pigeon describing the end then leapt out. She said to tell you that she loves you, Queen Eleanor of Vanalon."

There was dead silence in the room.

Xander hung his head, and Garth Stone looked down. "No," Eleanor moaned, tears streaming down her cheeks. Chip stood up and went to her. His own heart felt great loss at the passing of Queen Charlotte, who was like a mother to him. The new queen reached for him, burying her head in his shoulder. Balor stood up, clearing his throat.

"That will be all for today." He looked at Xander. "My brother and I have also experienced great sorrow in this war. I fear much more will come. On behalf of the Wizard's Guild, I offer our deepest condolences for your loss, Queen Eleanor. I knew your mother during her training. She was a fine pupil and an even greater monarch. We will miss her. Please take time to mourn, but understand that the best way you can honour her legacy is to stand up and fight the darkness that is coming. I have been preparing for three thousand years. The end times are here. We must train and be ready for the Last Battle. We can fight it, but in the end, we have no choice but to accept our fate."

He turned to the boy. "I uphold your title, Chip Oathbinder, Guardian of Humanity, and yours, Queen Eleanor of Vanalon. I urge you both to prepare for what is coming." He signalled for the others to leave. "Stay as long as you wish. The room is yours."

He exited with his Protector Maxim and Grand Wizard Skylar in tow. The Seer wanted to put the Galad Prophecy away, but the High Wizard shook his head. Xander and Garth stopped before Eleanor, offering the queen their condolences, and left the room.

Queen Eleanor held Chip for a long time, weeping bitterly. She began to speak of her memories. Chip listened to her stories, remembering how instrumental Queen Charlotte was in his upbringing, even his survival. He knew Eleanor was processing her incredible loss, cherishing the good memories, and buttressing herself to face the future. She released him to walk around the room. The new queen's eyes were wet, but she seemed to have regained some strength. They both realized that the Galad Prophecy was still on the table and walked over to look at it.

"We could destroy this darn prophecy right now," Chip said, clenching his fist. "I want to."

"I wish it were that easy," Eleanor sighed. She turned to him. "You must accept what is." He started shaking his head. "No, please. Look at me. If I die, you must accept it." Again, he began to protest. "Please. Let me go. If it is meant to be, so be it. Look at me. I love you."

Tears filled his eyes. "I love you too. I want to be with you longer than this. I want to be with you forever. You cannot die." The boy stood trembling before her, tears rolling down his cheeks.

"I will be with my mother. I will wait for you." She looked at him with love, cupping his cheeks and drawing him in to wipe away his tears. "You are the Guardian of Humanity. You have a great duty." Chip nodded with sadness. "Do it for me." She brought him close, kissed him, and rested her head on his shoulder. They held each other for a long time.

5

The cleric was waiting for them when they left the council room. "I have been instructed to take you to the Brown Level Wing, Queen Eleanor." He looked at Chip. "Skylar has asked that you be escorted to the Blue Wing."

The boy shook his head. "I go where she goes."

The cleric's eyes widened. "My instructions from Grand Wizard Skylar…"

"This is not up for debate. I am the Guardian of Humanity. My orders supersede Skylar's, and to be honest, everyone else's in Amrika except High King Dominor and the High Wizard himself. Her safety is my prime concern. Now, please escort us to the Brown Wing."

The cleric gaped, unsure what to do, then nodded. "Follow me, Guardian and Queen." They traversed the immense Blue Hall and exited in front of the massive gates. Chip marvelled at the size of everything. It was as if a race of giants placed the statues and walls up and then filled them with tiny humans. He looked up at the towering Brown Wing statue of a woman wizard, raising her finger to the sky.

"What is she pointing at?" Chip asked the cleric, who followed his gaze.

"All statues point to the Creator, believed to be the source of our Power," the man recited.

"How long have you been here?"

The cleric pushed his glasses up, scrunching his face in calculation. "Three hundred and fifty-three years. I am only at the Green Level, so I will unlikely make five hundred." He shrugged. "Time goes so fast."

Chip and Eleanor looked at each other, trying not to laugh. They crossed the empty area before the gates to the immense brown doors leading underneath the statue. It turned out the Brown Hall was identical to the Blue Hall, except it was less lavish and had more students and wizards. They began crossing the huge space.

"How many wizards are here?" Chip asked.

"In the Guild, we have less than five hundred. Remember that many are not Certified yet, but I am including them. Most are Yellow and Green. There are forty-seven Browns, twelve Blues, and...you." He looked at the boy in wonder. "I felt your...Power...in the council room. I could not believe it. You are truly the Guardian. Balor is very strict, but I believe he means well. I hope you can save us all." The man looked down, shy that he had said so much.

"I will try," Chip responded. They passed several large rooms off the hall, which looked like they were used for lessons.

Noticing his gaze, the cleric commented. "Those are classrooms. The teachers impart knowledge of Power, magical theory, history, and other traditional subjects such as math and English. Balor believes wizards should be educated to provide a valuable service to the public and the monarchs. He trains us to be learned advisors, not sideshow magicians. Those who do not take their studies seriously or fail the Trials are banished from the Guild."

"Are they barred from using their Power?" the queen asked.

The cleric looked surprised for a moment, then nodded, grimacing. "Yes. It is a bone of contention, even among the council members, but the High Wizard is adamant that those who cannot control themselves should not have access to Power."

Chip considered the man's words, knowing Xander's view on the subject. "How do you feel about that?" he asked.

The cleric looked apprehensive and sighed. "I am not in a position to comment on such matters, but I have heard that those barred from the Power eventually go mad."

Chip's eyes widened. "That sounds like torture," he said. The cleric looked at him but did not respond. Instead, he turned left and ascended a large marble staircase that bisected the hall at precisely the halfway point. They followed him up many steps to the second level, which opened into a massive dining hall.

In the middle sat a large wooden table that could comfortably seat over one hundred students.

"This is where the meals are served. A bell will toll when food is ready. Yellows and Greens prepare and serve the meals for the Browns and Blues. The High Wizard believes these two latter groups, limited in numbers, should focus solely on their training. They are exempt from chores. Once they are Certified, the graduates may stay here to fulfill certain roles or be sent as emissaries to the various cities to advise royalty and other forms of administration. The cities pay us a tithe to provide these services. Let me briefly show you the colonnade on the fortress wall then your rooms. I do not want you to be late for dinner. Tardiness is not accepted at the Guild."

The cleric walked across the dining hall to a row of open doors lining the entire southern side of the room and led them out to the top of the wall. When they reached the crenellated edge, the Guardian and queen gasped. The view was nothing short of remarkable. They could see the bridge they rode over with the unicorns across the vast green expanse of the front lawn. The Ancient Forest covered the whole horizon in a beautiful display of greenery. The immense trees rose even higher than the two-hundred-foot wall they stood on. The boy looked up to marvel at the giant statues, which extended another eight hundred feet into the air. Chip wanted to climb to the top and see the view.

The cleric followed his gaze and chuckled. "When I first arrived, I wanted to reach the tip of the finger too. It is a view like no other. I, however, am the wrong person for the job. I'm afraid my knees would protest. One of the younger Browns will be happy to take you there. Come. Let me show you to your rooms."

They started walking back towards the dining hall. The colonnade or road across the top of the wall was at least fifty feet across, extending over the front gates to the giant blue statue two thousand feet away. Wizards and students wearing different coloured robes were chatting in small groups or going for a walk. Some sat on benches reading books. Several pointed him out to others.

Chip heard someone call his name. Two blond wizards in blue robes emerged from a cluster of students talking animatedly over the front gates. He instantly recognized Thomas and Kristan. They hurried over, faces beaming.

"Enjoying the view?" Thomas asked, smiling. "I see you have met our cleric."

The old man bowed, acknowledging them. "What are you rascals up to?"

The twins both assumed an expression of mock injury.

"We are simply trying to live up to the lofty expectations of the Wizard's Guild," Kristan said innocently.

The cleric grunted. "Well, you are failing. How the two of you got Certified is beyond me." The old man tried not to grin.

Thomas held his heart as if he had been stabbed. "It is not our fault. Trouble finds us, I'm afraid." The blonde twin turned to the new recruits. "Sorry to interrupt the tour but we are curious which Level you are being placed at?"

The twins leaned in. "I am a Brown," Eleanor said. They nodded approvingly and then looked at Chip. It was obvious they were hoping he would be placed in the Blue Wing with them.

"I'm staying with her."

Their faces dropped. "We were hoping you were at the Blue Level given that you are the Guardian, whatever that means."

The cleric started laughing. Kristan looked at him with suspicion.

"What is so funny?" the twin asked.

"He chose the Brown Level. That is all I can say."

"He cannot choose where he goes. It does not work that way." Kristan turned to Chip. "What Level are you really? None of the monikers introducing you indicate your Level." Eleanor covered her mouth, trying not to smirk.

"There is no tower for me, so I chose Brown. I wish to be with the queen to watch over her," Chip said truthfully.

"Queen? I thought you were a... princess." Thomas interjected and then saw a look of sadness on her face. "Oh...I..."

"Her mother has passed," Chip said quietly.

Both twins bowed low. "We offer our deepest condolences," they said as one.

Eleanor nodded. "Thank you. I...need some time."

"Of course if you need anything, we are here. You two are just across the two-thousand-foot walkway," Kristan offered as if they were neighbours. He looked at Chip. "By the way, don't be ashamed if you do not have any magic. You are probably a fantastic swordsman or something. Being a Guardian sounds important, so I am happy they permit you to stay with the other magic wielders. We can talk later." Chip was about to comment, but the twins started walking back to the cluster of wizards they had talked to earlier.

The cleric looked at them and laughed, shaking his head. "If they only knew. In due time. Please follow me." He led them back into the dining hall and turned right, proceeding to the far end. The man opened two bronze doors into a foyer with stairs leading upwards. "We are now in the robes of the statue. This is where the bedroom suites are located. Come."

They mounted another two flights of marble stairs and reached a large common room with couches and tables. Shelves filled with books and board games lined the walls. Students in brown robes sat and talked in groups or read quietly. Most looked around their age. A severe woman in brown robes with a white border at the cuffs sat at a large desk overlooking the room. She had a long nose and gray hair pulled back tightly in a bun. The cleric brought them before her and bowed.

"Miss Highbrow. I have two new students to be assigned rooms."

She looked down her nose at him, glaring. "I was told there was to be only one student. I already filled two rooms earlier today. This is unprecedented." The woman looked at the two students sitting on the couch. It was Mina and Siz. They both waved excitedly at them. Chip grinned, and Eleanor waved back. Miss Highbrow looked at the exchange and sniffed. "I see you know each other. I trust this will not be a problem. Browns are required to display exemplary behaviour at all times. Now, where did this second student come from?"

The cleric tried to explain. "This is Chip Oathbinder. He has chosen to stay in the Brown Wing to be close to Queen Eleanor..."

"Let me stop you right there, cleric." Miss Highbrow raised her hand. "People do not choose to go anywhere. They are assigned." She looked at Eleanor. "I want to make it clear to you that your title of queen gives you no rank at the Guild. I have advised many 'queens' over the years as part of my duties and, frankly, do not feel they are better than anyone else. Worse, usually."

"I agree," Eleanor said. "I am not fond of the ones I have met in the other royal courts. I expect no special treatment."

"Good." Miss Highbrow turned to Chip. "What Level are you?"

The cleric interjected, "The High Wizard gave him the title of Guardian of Humanity, and he chose to stay in the Brown Wing."

"I am in charge of the Brown Wing. I do not recognize this title. Why is he not being placed according to his Level," she asked, her expression turning even more severe.

"They will all see the Assessor tomorrow, including the other two. Right now, we are going on their word," the cleric responded. "They came late today."

She snorted indignantly.

Chip stepped forward. "I am sorry for the confusion, Miss Highbrow. I am the Guardian of Humanity, assigned such a role by Grand Wizard Xandrostika and validated by the High Wizard. It puts me in rank below Dominor and Balor only." He noticed her sharp intake of breath when he called them by their first names. "I do not wish to use my title to get any special privileges, with the exception of my request to stay with the queen in the Brown Wing. This request is non-negotiable."

Miss Highbrow stared at him, mouth open. She looked at the cleric. "Do you vouch for this?" she demanded.

"I do," the old man said, meeting her gaze.

She pursed her lips. "Very well. For now, I will go along with this under protest. I will speak to the High Wizard myself during the next meeting. Follow me." She reached into the drawers of her large desk and pulled out two keys.

"One key is fine..." Chip started saying but stopped when the woman turned around with a snarl.

"I will give you each a room beside one another, again under protest. A boy and a girl in the same room is..." She struggled for the words, trying not to vomit, then gave him a severe gaze. "That is non-negotiable."

"Two rooms are fine," Eleanor said, holding her hands out in a placating manner. Miss Highbrow looked at her then sniffed again and turned around, mumbling about the nerve of the younger generation. The queen glanced at Chip, who was covering his mouth. She tried to punch him, but he dodged it. The cleric rolled his eyes.

They followed Miss Highbrow across the common room through large double doors down a wide hall with bedrooms on both sides. Most doors were open, revealing large, beautifully furnished rooms with four-poster beds. Rich paintings hung on the walls, and the wooden floors held large, plush throw rugs. The washrooms labelled for each sex were at the end of the hall. If this was the level of opulence in the Brown Wing, Chip could only wonder at the Blue.

Near the end of the wing, she handed Eleanor a key. "This is your room. Do not lose the key." She pointed at the boy and held out a second key. "This is yours next door. If you must go into her room, leave the door open. I do not know what game you are playing here, but I will find out. Dinner is in short order."

With that, she turned and walked rigidly back down the hall.

The cleric looked after her. "Not the most pleasant woman, but then again, she is the Brown Wing Leader." He paused as if that would explain it all. "Well, I must return to my post. If you need anything, do not hesitate." They thanked him, and he bowed low before taking leave. They looked at each other.

"Let me see your room," Chip said excitedly. She fumbled with her key and inserted it into the door.

"I do not want to get in trouble on my first day," she whispered.

"Then leave it open," he said with a smile, pushing on the door after hearing a click. They entered to find the room's design similar to the others. A polished wooden desk ran along the side wall, but the centerpiece was the luxurious four-poster bed.

"Go get ready," she said.

"In one moment, My Queen," he saluted. "Just waiting for you to give me something."

She smiled, looked around, and gave him a quick kiss. He pretended to be surprised, as if that was not what he wanted, then smiled and ran to his room. It was identical to hers.

"Let's go," Eleanor said almost immediately, popping her head around his doorframe. "I do not want to be late for dinner." He nodded, dropped off his things, and emerged from his room, shutting the door.

The couple re-entered the common room, finding Siz beaming. Mina was smiling as wide as she could, making her look odd. They walked over to the large divan and sat down, happy it was as comfortable as it looked.

"How are things going?" the queen asked.

"Great!" Siz answered first. "This place is amazing. Have you gone down to the yard yet?" They shook their heads. "It's huge. The bedrooms are beautiful. We are starting our training tomorrow after we get Assessed. What about you?"

"We had a meeting with the High Wizard," Eleanor said.

Siz and Mina looked at them wide-eyed.

"What was he like?" Mina asked curiously.

"Strict," Chip said. "He tests you a lot."

"What did you talk about?" asked Siz.

"I am sorry, but we cannot discuss that yet," Chip said as a loud, deep bell rang thrice. He could feel it in his chest.

"Let's go," Siz squealed. "I'm so hungry."

They went down the stairs and entered the dining hall. Chip noticed Miss Highbrow, who sat at a small desk off to the side, watching them with narrowed eyes. The huge dining table was laden with all manner of food. Several Yellows and Greens were walking to and fro, serving trays.

"Where do we sit?" Chip whispered to one of the servers, a girl in a yellow robe.

"Anywhere, sir," she said, blushing. "Meals are first come, first serve." She set down a tray full of pies and scurried away. The boy pulled out a chair for Eleanor and took one for himself. Siz and Mina sat beside them. They all looked astonished at the smorgasbord of culinary delights, even the queen. Chip tried to sample as many as he could before more food arrived.

"They will keep bringing food until you leave the table," the serving girl whispered in his ear. He turned to look at her, but she had already moved away. He glanced at the queen, who arched an eyebrow.

Chip shrugged and helped himself to roast duck. There were many other birds, including pheasant, quail, chicken, and turkey. For meat lovers, the choices were equally broad. Pork, beef, and goat were the ones he could readily identify, but there were others. Vegetables came steamed, braised, and grilled in many varieties. Pies and cakes were passed around frequently. Some students only ate from the dessert trays. Siz preferred those, betraying his sweet tooth. They ate long and heartily, sharing stories and poking fun at one another. The table was only half-full.

"Why are there so many empty chairs?" he asked the server girl.

"The Guild always ensures they will never be short a spot. They like to double the chairs depending on the number of students. Also, many magic wielders are being ordered to the Guild to help fight the war, so we get new arrivals every day. Today alone, we had you four. Can I ask you something?"

"Yes, no problem," he answered.

"Is it true that you did all those things that Grand Wizard Xander announced at the gates?"

He looked at her, sighing. "Yes, it is all true. There's no sense in denying it. I do not want attention, though. I want to be like everybody else." Her eyes widened.

"Yes, Mr. Guardian." She hurried away with a tray full of empty dishes.

"Got that, Mr. Guardian?" Eleanor laughed, poking him. He looked over, happy she was in good spirits.

He was about to respond when a deeper-sounding bell rang ten times.

Miss Highbrow stood up from her desk at the end of the room. "Emergency meeting, students. Everybody to the yard. Stand with your Wing."

The four looked at each other and then followed the other students. Chip noticed several people glancing at him, then whispering amongst themselves. He knew he had better get used to it. They all descended the stairs before funnelling into the great hall at the bottom. The students walked to large doors on the north side, which led to the yard. The setting sun gave everything a dark orange hue.

The other Levels were streaming out from their wings. Everybody spread out, listening to their Wing Leaders until five hundred students were arrayed in front of a large podium. Standing in the middle of the dais was High Wizard Balor.

Behind him, the Wing Leaders took their seats, one from each Level. They sported robes embroidered with white thread at the cuffs. Miss Highbrow sat in the Brown chair. Xander and Skylar were standing on either end of the High Wizard. Garth Stone stood to the side with several other Protectors, watching the events impassively.

"Ladies and gentlemen," Balor began. His eyes blazed an incredible blue as he used his Power to project his voice over the crowd. The noise immediately died down. "I have grave news. The City of Vanalon has fallen to the demon army, which now marches on

Calgar. We have seen this coming for several weeks, some of us much longer. The barrier my father, the High Wizard Arkan, and many others erected to imprison the Demon King is failing fast."

He continued in a strong voice, "Today, we received some honoured guests and students." Chip heard Siz puff out his chest, waiting to be announced. Mina and Eleanor both noticed his reaction, trying not to laugh. "For those who witnessed their arrival at the gates, many names of introduction, called monikers, were used." He paused for dramatic effect. "They were all correct." Gasps went through the crowd. It was clear many had believed the claims exaggerated.

"My brother, Grand Wizard Xander, stands beside me. Over there stands the Guardian of Humanity. He is young but determined, like many of you. Next to him is the newly crowned Queen Eleanor of Vanalon. We offer deep condolences for the loss of her mother, Queen Charlotte, who fell in battle."

Sad intakes of breath went through the crowd and whispered prayers to the Creator.

"When Calgar falls, the demon hordes will eventually march on Toron, with their dark master leading them. Before attacking the capital, the foul creatures will likely await his arrival in Cave Mountain, the Demon King's ancestral home. This means we have some time after Calgar falls, though much less than I had hoped. I am not privy to the ways of the Creator or the Balance. I am open to prophecy, but in the end I use my three millennia of experience to make decisions after consulting my advisors. If we get this wrong, we all die. The end of times is indeed upon us. The Last Battle is coming. We are only a day's ride north of Toron. We can provide aid quickly, but we are not ready. Many of you have not even received your Certification.

"For the first time in the Guild's history, I will do away with your instruction and elective courses. Before this, to be Certified, you needed to pass all five Trials and complete a full course load of subjects, all within a five-year time limit. Now, you only need to pass your five Trials. If you fail any Trial three times, you will be barred from your Power and sent home."

Shocked whispers went through the crowd. Some students looked scared.

Balor continued, ignoring the chatter, "We need warrior wizards now, successful magic wielders. I have been at odds with many over barring students. My goal has always been, and will always be, the safety and protection of Amrika. I will not send out or allow a failed student to misuse their Power and threaten others. If they cannot control themselves through mastery of their gift, how can I, in good conscience, send them into the world to protect others? Untrained or failed magic wielders will abuse or misuse their Power, and I will not stand for it.

"The stark truth is some of you do not deserve your gift. If you believe you do, work hard and earn it. Show your instructors you have control over your Power. When you pass the Trials and receive your Certification, report to Grand Wizard Skylar so we can assign you a task for the upcoming war. As of tomorrow, anyone can take a Trial in the yard. If you fail one, go to the head instructor in your hall, review the material, then practice. Do not retake the test until you are confident you have mastered the skills required. Each Level has a different standard or minimum that needs to be achieved. The Wing Leaders or Higher Level trusted graduates will supervise the first four Trials. I will personally be in charge of the fifth and final Trial. It is the Trial of Fear and the most important. If we cannot master our fears, we have no control."

More murmurs went through the students.

The High Wizard raised his hands. "If the barrier fell today, the Demon King could reach Toron within a month. I give you that long to pass the Trials." Shouts of shock rang out in the crowd. Some students wailed. Balor ignored them, holding up his hand. "The one-month deadline begins now. You must pass, or else you are a liability. I cannot risk the safety of other wielders and the citizens of Amrika with wizards who cannot control their Power. My views will not be swayed. All Certified wizards will be available during training hours to assist students who ask for help. We need to build an army. We are counting on you. Emissaries have been sent to the other races to garner their assistance.

"Unlike humans, every Dark Elf has the Power. I do not know how many are still hidden behind the barrier. It could be hundreds or even thousands. We need all the races to come together, including the Light Elves, to stand a chance. Our council is poring over the histories to find the missing Light Elves. Those who are Certified can assist in this endeavour. There is much work to be done. To our would-be Protectors, no one can be trained in a month. Your physical skills can only be honed over many years of practice. The Final Test for a Protector is arduous. If you have not trained diligently for at least three years, I recommend you enlist in Toron. For those who have passed the Final Test and are not sworn to a wizard, see master trainer Maxim to be assigned.

"I am happy to announce that the Silver Sword tournament set for month's end will take place three days from today and run for one week. Only those who have passed the Final Test can enter. Chase Longfellow, trained under the Weapons Master Garth Stone, has accepted a challenge to fight our current champion, Maxim's student, Carvor." Cheers erupted in the crowd. Balor continued. "I felt the best way to do this was in tournament style. Chase will need to pass his Final Test to enter the tournament, but based on my brother's assertions, this should not be a problem.

"For those wizards who need a break from practice, this tournament should provide a welcome respite. After the winner is crowned at the end of the tournament, we will hold one more match." He paused, watching as the students tried to figure out who would be the contestants. "In a rematch two decades in the making, I would see my Protector, Master Trainer Maxim, take on the most decorated Weapons Master of all time, my brother's Protector, Garth Stone."

There was a dramatic pause as the crowd digested the enormity of the match, and then loud cheers erupted. The Protectors gathered at the side of the stage raised their swords, displaying a rare show of enthusiasm. Chip looked at Garth, whose face looked chiselled from granite. Judging by the students' excitement, it was apparent the tournament was a sought-after spectacle. A rematch of the great legends elevated that fervour to a new level.

"Finally, I have reinstated the Wizard's Duel Tournament, beginning tomorrow, lasting eight days." Xander looked up sharply at this announcement. Balor noticed his brother's reaction and smiled. "Do not worry. Safeguards are in place, and healers will be standing by." He looked at the assembly of students. "This tournament was cancelled after the Great Battle as it was deemed too brutal, resulting in the deaths of several wizards. It was a new time of peace and considered unnecessary. Back then, wizard fire was allowed, which caused burns so severe that the healers could not save some in time.

"This new format bans the use of such fire and has rules. It is straightforward. Simply push your opponent out of the Wizard's Circle. You can use any means necessary other than wizard's fire, and any force must not be a killing blow. Wizards need to test their relative strength against peers. You will see that some can defeat a Higher Level with speed and accuracy. The rules are as such: You can only duel once a day. If you issue a challenge and it is accepted, you must duel. If it is declined, you are declared the winner by default. You must issue one challenge or accept a challenge each day to stay in the tournament. You must duel by the setting sun. You will see by mathematics that, starting with five hundred students and halving them each day, only two will be left by the eighth day.

"Students who lose or decline a challenge are out of the tournament and cannot be challenged again. Their names will be recorded in the duel book as a loss. You can only challenge someone one Level above or below you, not two, unless we are down to the final thirty-two combatants. I will not force anyone to enter this tournament, but refusing to duel will factor into your placement if you pass the Trials. This will be excellent training for real combat. After all, Protectors hone their skills by sparring. Duels will give magic wielders experience. I want you to become warrior wizards. The first set of duels begins tomorrow. Challenges begin now. Rest well tonight. I look forward to fighting alongside you in the Last Battle."

The High Wizard raised his hands to deafening applause.

6

The students milled about, breaking off into clusters. Many appeared anxious about the upcoming Trials, while others expressed relief that the academic portions had been removed.

Chip noticed most students were around his age, though looks could be deceiving. He knew that their age slowed considerably once the Power manifested in a magic wielder. The Higher-Level wizards aged incredibly slowly. The twins were in their late thirties but looked like young adults or older teenagers.

He glanced at Eleanor, who was whispering with Mina. It looked like the small girl was coming out of her shell. Siz stood to the side, looking nervous.

"What's wrong?" Chip asked, moving closer.

"I'm scared about the Trials. I don't do well on tests," Siz admitted, looking down. "In Thundar, the students in my school would make fun of me when I failed. After I found my Power, I hurt some of them and got kicked out. I only came here because the magistrate ordered me. My dad wants me to be a fisherman, but I get seasick easily. I don't even like seafood. If I fail the Trials, I don't know what I will do."

"Then, do not fail. Tomorrow, we will get Assessed, whatever that means, and then we will see what the First Trial is about. The weapons master always told me that fighting is easy if you've practiced enough. It will be the same for the Trials," he assured him.

Chip heard a commotion and turned to see a group of students wearing brown robes pushing through the throng to stand before him. They all seemed his age, but who knew? An older-looking, burly boy stood in the front, appraising him.

"Are you the Guardian?"

"Yes, they call me that," Chip answered, taking in the threatening stance and contemptuous tone. Immediately, he thought of Rupert's old friends Gunter, Biff, and Chubs.

"Did you really slay a dragon? Kill demons? Defeat the Demon King's general?" he asked with a sneer. "You don't look very tough." The others behind him snickered.

Chip found it ironic that he was just having a conversation with Siz about bullying, and this fool was trying to impress his friends by putting him down. He was not in the mood.

"What is your name?" Chip asked without preamble.

"Gob," he said. "Why?"

"I'm challenging you to a duel," Chip announced in a loud voice. Gob blinked. Others started gathering around.

"Duels don't start until tomorrow," the large boy said, spitting on the grass.

"That's correct, but the High Wizard said challenges start now. Are you scared?" he asked. "I thought you were trying to impress your friends. I tell you what. I'm trained in hand-to-hand fighting too, plus most weapons, and I'm pretty good at magic. I will challenge you on any one you want." A larger crowd had gathered, including the Blue Level twins. Siz was watching slack-jawed, not sure what to do.

Gob looked Chip up and down, realizing he held a considerable size advantage over the Guardian. He cracked his knuckles. "I'm from Flod, in the far south, near the swamps. We wrestle crocs. You're gonna be in for a whipping if you talking fisticuffs. I can also filet an alligator with my dagger in under a minute. I'm one of the strongest Browns in the Guild." His friends showed surprise, then grinned and nodded, slapping him on the back. Chip could tell he was lying, at least about the last part.

One of his friends, an even bigger student in the group, urged him on. "Look how small he is, Gob. You won't need me on this one," he grunted like a pig.

"I can take care of this runt myself, Bart," Gob laughed, flexing his arms.

"Well, that's just swell, Gob." Chip nodded. "Does that mean you will accept all my challenges?"

He smiled warmly. Something about his confidence gave the burly boy pause. Gob started pacing back and forth, whipping himself into a frenzy.

The twins fist-pumped the air. "Kick his ass, Chip!" Kristan yelled.

"Slap him silly!" hollered Thomas.

"Let's see what this Guardian is made of!" a young blond boy in green robes shouted.

"Gob and his friends fight dirty," Jordy yelled, appearing through the crowd.

"I accept all challenges," Gob bellowed. Everyone cheered. The large boy started advancing on Chip, who placed his left foot forward, pointing his toe slightly inward as trained.

"What is the meaning of this?" Miss Highbrow pushed into the group. She looked at them in shock. "Wizards do not fight physically. That is why we have Protectors. I am not supportive of these barbaric...duels, but I have no say in the matter. I do, however, forbid you from physical combat."

"Now, now. We have healers here," Grand Wizard Skylar said slyly, joining them. "When I was a young wizard, fisticuffs were common. You are not suggesting I am barbaric, are you Miss Highbrow?" The old man turned to her with an evil smile.

"Why, of course not, Grand Wizard. I just felt..." She trailed off, seeing his expression. Garth and Chase arrived, standing at the front. Almost at the same time, Maxim and a heavily muscled young man appeared on the other side.

"Ah, Maxim and Carvor, would you mind refereeing a physical duel of fisticuffs between these young lads?" asked Skylar.

"As you wish, Grand Wizard," Maxim said shortly.

Chip knew Skylar did not like him and assumed he had no fighting skills. He looked at Garth, who betrayed a hint of a smile.

"Let's go, Guardian," Chase yelled. A few in the crowd took up the cheer, then more picked it up.

Gob began circling Chip, who handed off the pouch with the egg in it to Eleanor and unbuckled his sword, doing the same. He then assumed his hand-to-hand combat stance, turning with the burly boy. A huge crowd had gathered around the two combatants. Chip noticed Grand Wizard Balor watching intently from the podium.

Gob suddenly ran at him, bringing his right hand around in a vicious hook aimed at the boy's temple. Chip smoothly ducked, appearing to the side of the bigger boy and, using his whole body, unleashed a right uppercut to his ribs. There was a slight pop, and he immediately followed it with a right-turning kick to Gob's exposed abdomen. Chip assumed his stance again, waiting for the next attack.

The large boy doubled over, holding his side, then charged again, not wishing to show weakness. This time, he dived low, intent on grabbing the Guardian around the waist and landing on top of him. Almost counterintuitively, Chip charged forward as trained, jumping up and driving his right knee with all his power straight into Gob's face. There was a sickening squelch as his nose shattered, and the impact drove his head straight up, blood leaking profusely from his nostrils.

Gob staggered around, dazed. Chip planted his feet and unleashed a full-force right hook square on the bigger boy's chin, which snapped his head sideways, causing his whole body to spin around and seize up before falling backwards on the ground. Cheers went up in the crowd then a gasp.

Chip felt something connect with the side of his head. The world wobbled, and he knew from training to escape the situation. He rolled forward, feeling something very heavy land on him. For some reason, his mind immediately thought of the immense wave of stone pressing on his back at Cave Mountain. A claustrophobic fear clutched at him, which he immediately replaced with rage.

Without thinking, he broke through the Wall and seized his Power, surrounding himself. The weight lifted off his back, and he leapt up, spinning around. His eyes blazed a ferocious red. The bigger student, Bart, was rubbing his face, which had burn marks on it. The crowd fell back in shock. Gasps and screams erupted.

"He has red eyes!" an older lad yelled in disbelief.

"Dear Creator!" a girl screamed.

"This kid is so cool!" shouted the blond, green-robed boy from before.

Bart stared at his hands, which were burnt too, then looked at Chip with rage. His eyes suddenly blazed a pale brown, and he lifted his hands, shooting a weak stream of wizard's fire at the boy's chest. Chip did not even bother to form a shield. He wrapped himself in a thicker envelope of red magic and walked towards the large student. Realizing his fire was having no effect, Bart tried to turn and run, but Chip seized him with his Power. Lifting his hand, the orphan threw the bully into the air with frightening force. His large body sailed up and up, going higher until he was above the walls.

The crowd went dead silent. Every neck craned skyward, waiting to see how high he would go. Long moments passed as Bart finally reached the apex of his flight, stopping briefly in mid-air and then slowly falling back to Earth. He picked up speed during his descent, and a thin, high-pitched scream grew in volume as he fell towards the ground.

Chip wanted to let him go, then sighed and held out his hand at the last moment, stopping him inches from the ground. Bart was hanging upside down with a large, wet stain on his crotch. He began blubbering for mercy, to which the crowd finally responded, laughing and pointing. Chip grinned, dropping him on his friend Gob, then released his Power.

The students cheered, and some broke into applause. Miss Highbrow stared at Chip as if he was the Demon King himself. Grand Wizard Skylar gave him a grudging nod and walked away.

Chase came over, grinning. "You've gotten a bit slower but not bad overall," he assessed.

"Well, I haven't trained in over a month. My kick was a little weaker than I would have liked. Nothing I couldn't handle, though," he laughed. "I did not expect the sucker punch. I had this view that all wizards were honourable. Looks like they are the same as everybody else."

Other students were crowding around, congratulating him. He did not know if he had done the right thing, but Chip was tired of bullies. He looked at Siz, who had a look of wonder on his face.

"Well, that's one way to do it," the overweight boy said, shaking his head. "Wish I could do that."

"Keep training," Chip said. "Bullies are usually just big fools who do not train. They try to pick on those smaller and weaker. I'm tired of it, especially after your story."

Siz beamed. "Best thing I ever saw."

Eleanor came up with Mina beside her. "A little much, you think? Well, at least they know who you are now. You might have eliminated all challenges in one fell swoop."

Gob finally stood up, holding on to Bart for support. Chip went over and put his hand on both their shoulders. They turned around and shrank in fear, trying to pull away. He seized the Power, froze them, and sent healing energy throughout their bodies, mending their wounds. He let go and released his magic. They looked at him awkwardly, then Gob stuck out a meaty hand.

"I won't be accepting your challenge tomorrow. I've seen enough. Truce?" the big boy said sheepishly.

"Me too," Bart said. "Sorry for punching you."

Chip relented, shaking their hands. He knew how hard it was for someone to apologize and believed in second chances. "Apology accepted. Try to remember we are on the same side." They nodded and walked away.

"Why did your eyes go red?" Mina asked, watching them go. She still had a fearful look on her face.

"I honestly don't know. I was born this way. I suppose I am the balance to the Demon King," he said, shrugging.

She looked at him oddly, about to say something, and then Jordy rushed beside her.

"That was amazing. Trust me when I say they deserved it." Jordy slapped him on the back and smiled at Mina, who smiled in return.

The blond boy in the green robes ran up and gave the Guardian a light but quick punch on the shoulder. Chip raised his eyebrows. "That was awesome. I'm going to watch all your matches!" he exclaimed. Chip was about to tell the young-looking lad that he did not expect to have anymore, but the boy ran off.

The twins came up to them, still cheering.

"The Red Level? I can't believe it!" Kristan raved.

"I knew it all along," Thomas said, trying not to laugh and failing.

"You weren't joking when you said you were Red Level." Kristan grabbed Chip's shoulders in wonder, peering at his eyes.

"That was a story for the ages," Thomas gushed, throwing one hand up in the sky, re-enacting the event. "I have never seen someone fly before." He laughed, doubling over.

"Nice move, Guardian," Kristan added, trying to copy the jumping knee.

Two dark-haired girls in yellow robes came up. They seemed very new. "How did you do that?" one said, eyes wide.

"How many wizards have red eyes?" the other asked.

"Uh... just me so far," Chip said, not sure if they were serious.

They looked at him dreamily.

"Ahem," the queen said politely. The two girls snapped out of their infatuation, noticing her. "The other students are going back to the hall. Let's join them, shall we?" Eleanor said, taking his arm.

"Sounds good," Chip responded, saying goodbye. "I am pretty tired. It's been a long day."

"Bye!" the girls called as one, waving.

They returned to the Brown Hall and noticed that some students were already practicing magic in some of the large rooms off to the sides. Chip realized he had no idea what the Trials entailed, let alone required for practice. He decided he would tackle that tomorrow.

The princess wanted to go upstairs and relax on one of the couches. Some other students came over and introduced themselves, congratulating him. Several asked about the colour of his eyes, but he gave the same answer. Miss Highbrow sat behind her desk, trying to avoid everyone. The whole night seemed to have been a bit much for her. She reminded Chip of Miss Owl, but not as funny.

Mina started to engage in their conversations more, slowly breaking out of her shell. Siz introduced himself to others as the Guardian's friend, which garnered him attentive ears as he retold the events. He was able to weave himself into the story enough that it looked like he was at least partially responsible for winning the fights. Gob and Bart did not come out of their rooms.

Chip noticed the queen whispering with Mina, her face serious. Mina held her hands as a tear slid down Eleanor's cheek. He knew she was thinking about her mother again. Chip wondered sadly how many more he would lose by the end.

The boy walked over and put his arm around Eleanor's shoulders, letting her know he was there. They continued talking for a while, and then his eyes grew heavy. He noticed other students were heading for their rooms. Siz and Mina decided to stay up longer, so Chip, joined by Eleanor, bade them good night and departed. He walked the queen through the double doors and down the bedroom hall. In his mind, it felt odd thinking of her as a queen. She had always been the princess to him. She stopped at her door, noticing his expression.

"I cannot believe it either," she said. "My whole family is gone. I am not ready to be queen." Her lip trembled.

"I am here and always will be," he said, drawing her to him. She looked up into his green eyes. He kissed her softly. "Do not be sad, My Queen." Her eyes widened in surprise. He had never said that to her before, but it felt right. "You will rule Vanalon again one day. Your mother will not die in vain. I promise."

He looked at her with determination until she nodded and put her arms around him. After a long embrace, he kissed her good night, and they retired to their separate rooms.

In bed, Chip went over his memories of Queen Charlotte. Auntie Clare was like a mother to him, but ironically, Charlotte was like an aunt. He loved her dearly. A great feeling of sadness and loss overwhelmed him, and he wept. So many had already lost their lives, and this was only the beginning. How many more would die in the Last Battle? Would he lose all his friends? And what about her? What about the prophecy? His sorrow slowly turned to simmering anger, and his thoughts went dark with vengeance. It took him a while to fall asleep.

The next day began with a flurry of activity. The students chattered over breakfast about which Trials they would take that day. Many had already picked their favourites for the Protector and Wizard Tournaments. Most thought Carvor would easily defeat this newcomer, Chase. A few pointed out that Chase had been trained by the greatest weapons master of all time and sided with him.

Many saw Chip as the easy winner for the Wizard tournament, but the boy cautioned that he was still deciding what to do. He had nothing to prove by entering the tournament. An older girl named Nadine asked if he would deny a challenge, which he admitted he likely would not. This was due to his sense of honour and training competitiveness. Gob and Bart entered the dining hall midway through breakfast, and the room went silent.

Chip made it a point to stand up and greet them. "Good morning, gentlemen. Glad you could join us. How's it going?"

"Well, after the ass whooping we got yesterday, not too good, but my dada always said when you fall down, pick yerself back up." Gob smiled crookedly.

"We gonna watch the Protectors fight," Bart said, "Try to pick up a few pointers. I know we need them. Are you dueling today, Guardian?"

"Honestly, I don't have to because Gob refused the challenge. They will mark me as a win. I want to see what the Trials are about anyway," Chip responded.

"Well, I sure feel sorry for yer next challenger." Gob grinned. They all laughed, and the two burly boys sat at the table's end. Breakfast consisted of eggs, bacon, fried potatoes, pancakes with syrup, egg-battered toast, fruits, tarts, and whipped cream. They washed it down with a ginger, lemon, and honey morning drink called "Charge," a favourite among wizards.

When finished, they headed down to the yard. An assorted group of students followed them, trying to see what the Guardian would do next. Stories of his exploits, especially after yesterday's fight, grew to new proportions. One student asked if it was true that he floated a whole mountain across the plains. He laughed too hard to answer but did manage to shake his head from side to side.

When they arrived in the immense courtyard, they saw a large white circle on the south side of the enormous field, in front of the podium. On the far side was a newly constructed, rectangular-shaped dirt arena with railings. Seats were arranged behind each rail ten rows deep, with each successive row raised higher than the last to provide everyone with a clear view.

Several Protectors were warming up on the dirt floor, doing various exercises. He did not see Chase or Xander. The five Trials were spread around the vast courtyard at even intervals. Chip had learned from other students that they could all be challenging in different ways. The Fifth Trial was the hardest, supervised by Balor himself. His section, located at the far end of the yard in a white pavilion, stood closed as admittance required an appointment.

Eleanor pointed to the side of the podium where a man in a multi-coloured robe sat at a large wooden desk. "That is the Assessor. Miss Highbrow said he would be the only one wearing all the colours and that we must see him this morning." Behind the man, oddly enough, were stairs going down into the ground under the podium. They had not noticed them the evening before.

"Let's go," Chip said.

They approached the Assessor, who was busy reviewing a list of names. His hair shone bright white, standing in all directions. He looked up, lowering his glasses. "Well, it's about time."

"Really," Chip said, playing along. "For what?"

"Don't be smart with me, young man, Guardian or not. Now, who's first?"

They all looked at each other. Siz and Mina stepped backwards.

"You!" the man said, pointing at Siz. "Front and center."

The overweight boy froze, unsure what to do. "Why?" he asked, grimacing, waiting for the rebuke.

It came swiftly. "To be Assessed. Are you daft, boy? Now stand front and center."

"Oh," Siz said faintly. He moved in front of the desk. The man waited.

"Well? I'm waiting," the Assessor said with a glare.

"Oh gosh. Don't get mad, but waiting for what?" Siz asked timidly.

"Good grief, you are daft. Did no one explain how this works?" He sighed. "Never mind. Show me your Power, and I will assign you a robe."

Siz nodded then shook his head. "Wait. What do I do with the Power?"

"May the Creator save me from ignorance," the man prayed then stared at the quavering boy. "Break your Wall so I can see your eyes. Got it?"

Siz nodded. He concentrated hard, and his eyes blazed a dark amber brown brightened with a hint of silver. The Assessor blinked. "What an odd colour. Then again, I assessed a boy at the Green Level yesterday with the same silver tinge. Strange times. Alright, young man, off you go." He handed him a piece of paper and jerked a thumb behind him.

"Um, go where?" Siz asked, already grimacing, anticipating another rebuke.

"By the grace of the Creator, you are a unique one. Go down the stairs, open the door, and the seamstress will fit you with a brown robe." He enunciated each instruction slowly as if talking to a small child. Siz nodded and ran down the stairs.

"Next!" the Assessor called. Mina looked around shyly then

stepped forward. The man peered at her through his glasses, wizened face scrunched.

"Display your Power," he ordered. She nodded, closed her eyes, and exhaled. When she opened them, a dark brown colour blazed forth.

The Assessor grunted, peering deep into her eyes. "What are you hiding in there," he murmured to himself. "Have you left your Wall down for long periods?" he asked. She shook her head, looking down. "Hmmm. You are fairly strong and mysterious." He scribbled something on a piece of paper. "Take this. Next." He waved her away. Siz was already walking back with a new brown robe, beaming. He seemed to like the way it fit. Chip noticed a small crowd gathered around them.

Eleanor stepped forward. The Assessor looked up, and his face softened. "My condolences, Queen of Vanalon. I knew your mother when I was a young man. She was a kind woman. Please, display your Power." The queen nodded, and her eyes blazed a ferocious brown, scattered with red chips.

The Assessor gasped. "Good grief. What is this?" He peered closer, mouth working. "In all my years, I have not seen such a thing. Did your Power always look like this?" Eleanor explained Chip's blood mixing with hers during healing. The Assessor sat back, exhaling. "Well, I'll be. I never thought that could work. High Wizard Balor will be interested in that, let me tell you. Even without the red spots, your Power would have been the strongest Brown I have ever seen. Now....who knows? I am tempted to put you in with the Blues, but there would be too much politics. Brown it is."

He scribbled and handed her a sheet of paper. Before she could take it, the Assessor shook his head, mumbled something, then pulled the paper back to scribble something else. She stood waiting, unsure what to do. Chip looked at her, trying not to laugh. The man studied the paper for a moment more then nodded to himself and handed it to her. Eleanor took it and headed for the stairs. The Assessor turned to look at the Guardian.

"Ah, the best for last? Come forward, boy. If the stories are true, I will be the first Assessor to see someone like you."

"What Level are you?" Chip asked curiously, stepping forward. Mina came back to join them, wearing a perfectly fitted brown robe. Eleanor had gone down the stairs.

The Assessor looked up sharply. "Why, I am no Level. I am an Assessor. I can discern shades and patterns in the colours that go into your report and help the Higher Level wizards decide how to assign you. We are the most powerful Sensers in the land. There is a whole school of training strictly for Assessors. Only one is chosen per lifetime."

"What happens to the others?" Chip asked.

"Hmmm. Inquisitive, are we? Interesting. The others become investigators of illegal magic and work for the Guild."

Chip's eyes widened. "Spies?"

"Ha, you are a bold one, boy. I suppose that makes sense. Spies is a strong word. It is essential that...strategic people be placed to ensure that no magic wielders run around abusing their Power. When identified, we simply invite them to the Guild to be trained or barred.

"And if they refuse?" Chip asked.

The old man's face tightened. "They cannot refuse. The higher the privilege, the higher the duty. They must and will be trained. It is the way."

"I have heard that before," Chip sighed, stepping forward. A large crowd had now gathered. He noticed the young blond boy in green robes from yesterday walking up, grinning at him and waving. "Very well, Assessor, assess away." Chip broke through his Wall, eyes blazing a bright red. Gasps erupted from the crowd.

The Assessor had a look of wonder on his face, like a small child. "It is beautiful," he breathed, leaning forward. "Come closer." Chip stepped right up to him. "Ah, yes, of course, what... Power." He shook his head then looked down. Chip waited for him to speak, but the old man did not move. The boy released his Power and stood awkwardly. Eleanor had returned wearing a lovely brown robe with red cuffs.

The other students looked at the queen in surprise and then whispered about her sleeves. She walked over to Chip and gave him a questioning look. He shrugged, nodding towards the Assessor, unsure what to do.

Suddenly, the old man's head snapped up. His eyes turned milky white. The Assessor's voice rose to a high pitch. It did not sound anything like him.

"The wasp will strike soon, chosen one. He knows you are here. The boy... green robe... If he reveals. Find three kings...Barrier falls soon." He choked, struggling to breathe. "He sees me!" the old man gasped. "He is too strong..."

The Assessor was having trouble breathing. Chip grabbed his hand and then felt a powerful jolt. Something immense and dark slithered into his consciousness. The boy seized his Power reflexively. Before him, crystal clear in his mind, stood the Demon King.

7

All the stories Chip had ever heard paled in comparison to the malevolence that stood before him. The Demon King's red eyes blazed through a black, horned helmet. A muscular body, rippling with red Power, stepped forward. His black cape trailed behind him. The boy instinctively knew the Calm would not contain this being.

"Bow!" the Unnamed One commanded.

A ridiculous pressure hit the orphan's back, forcing him down. Chip almost fell to his knees, but he resisted. The Guardian filled himself with his Power, then lifted his head, straining. The Dark Elf laughed, a sound like bones rubbing together. "You cannot defeat me, boy. Now bow!" The force increased further, and Chip strained with all his might. He looked the Demon King in his red eyes.

"No, Killian. I will not."

The boy unleashed all his magic into the figure, pushing him out. There was a moment of surprise in the Dark Elf's eyes at being named, and he flew backwards, out of the boy's mind and the Assessors. Chip wrapped them both in a heavy red shield, feeling the immense Power try to get in again, but it became weaker and finally dissipated. The boy looked around, realizing he had his arms around the old man, whose eyes had returned to normal.

The crowd stood in shocked silence. Siz looked scared, while Mina had an unreadable expression. He stepped back, releasing his Power, and staggered.

"He is gone now, Assessor. What happened?" Chip asked, trying to steady himself.

The old man looked at the boy in awe. "I received a Telling that showed me the barrier, and then... He entered my mind. He would have killed me."

"I do not doubt it. I am happy you are alright."

"I saw his eyes," the Assessor said with a trembling voice. "Yours were the strongest I have ever seen, but his... He is coming for you."

Chip sighed. "I gathered that." He looked at Eleanor. "I really need to find an Orb of Power or something." She laughed, and he smiled tiredly.

"It was nice to meet you finally, Guardian," the Assessor said, scribbling. He looked up and handed the boy a piece of paper.

Chip took it and nodded. "Why did you not say earlier that you had the Telling?"

The old man laughed. "Ha. If I did, I would spend all my days fortune-telling. No thanks. Next!"

Chip walked down the stairs under the podium. Eleanor waited outside. The door at the bottom opened to a long hall with rows of robes hanging on hooks along both sides. Strangely, they were not grouped by colour. An older, mouse-looking woman in yellow robes held out her hand, not saying a word. He gave her the piece of paper. She grabbed it with a bored look. The woman yawned as she read the writing then jerked her head up.

"You are the red-eyed one." She scrutinized him. "You...are not what I expected. Follow me." He decided he would take the comment as a compliment, though he knew that was unlikely. She seized her Power and scurried down the long hall, looking at both sides, turning her head. He walked fast to keep up. This continued until he wondered if they had reached the end of the yard and the Guild itself. Finally, she stopped.

"Ah, here we are." She beamed and pointed. He followed her finger, and at the end of the hall, a red robe hung on a hook by itself. He glanced at her with brows furrowed, wondering why she did not immediately lead him straight to it since it was the only red one. She looked at him, her eyes shining bright yellow, nose twitching. He decided not to ask and pulled the robe off its hook.

The material had a rich, luxurious feel. He pulled it over his clothes and felt it fall comfortably in place.

"I trust it fits well?" she asked squeakily.

He nodded. "It fits perfectly."

She smiled. "I know." The woman released her Power and hurried back down the long hall, looking back and forth as a mouse would. He could not help but grin.

Chip emerged back into the yard, receiving great applause from the large crowd. They got to see the red-eyed boy wizard all dressed up. Xander stood in the front, smiling. Chip waved at everyone and walked up to the old man.

"My goodness, you look great. It fits perfectly," Xander said in approval.

"Yes, I was surprised it would."

The wizard looked at him funny. "They all do."

"Huh."

"Never mind," the wizard pulled him aside. "I felt you use your magic. The Assessor filled me in. What did you experience?" Chip recounted the events. When he finished, the wizard's eyes went wide.

"I have heard of this before, though it is extremely rare. Sometimes, there is a Telling whereby the Seer talks about a certain individual or event, which can briefly provide a connection to it or them. If the being is very powerful or adept enough in magic, it can insert its presence in the Teller's mind, along with a good chunk of Power. They have a tiny window and need to do this quickly. I do not know how much of the Demon King's Power was able to come through, but I am happy you were able to cast him out."

"It was the most Power I have ever faced. I could not believe how strong he was." Chip shuddered. The wizard nodded.

"It is hard to say how much you felt. If he asked you to bow to him, the Demon King must have been confident he had sent enough. You may have surprised him," Xander added.

Chip took some solace in that. "The Assessor's Telling said I must find three kings, and the wasp will strike. I am not sure how it can enter the Guild, but I will be vigilant. He said the barrier is going to fall soon. Also, there's a boy in green robes that might reveal something. I think I know who he's talking about." Chip looked around. Sure enough, the blond boy stood watching at the front of the crowd. When he realized the Guardian had noticed him, he waved happily.

Chip beckoned him forward, and the lad looked around. He pointed at his chest to make sure it was him he wanted. When the Guardian nodded, he laughed and ran to stand before them. He was tall and skinny but looked younger than Chip. The boy wore a long green robe. He seemed happy and excited to be in the presence of the red-eyed Guardian.

"What is your name?" Xander asked.

"Ethrang. I gave it to myself when I was younger. I'm an orphan," the boy blurted, grinning. Something about him made Chip feel good. He seemed like a free spirit. Yet, there was something else too. He could not put his finger on it.

"How long have you had your Power?" the wizard asked.

Ethrang thought about it. "Over two years. I was fourteen summers when I found it."

"Then we are the same age, though you look younger," Chip said. "Makes sense. When did you get here?"

The blond boy laughed. "Same day as you, yesterday. I saw your fight. Nice moves, by the way."

"Where are you from?" Chip asked curiously.

Ethrang paused, considering his answer. He shrugged and said, "I'm from Banfar."

Xander and Chip shared a look. Something was not right about his story.

"If you came yesterday, then you must have been in Banfar when we were there. Do you remember us?" Chip asked.

The boy looked uncomfortable but quickly brushed it off. "Uh, yes. You are the Guardian. The whole city knows about you. I saw what you did to that Dark Elf in the Lower District. I thought it was amazing. I decided to tag along since I had nothing better to do. I can read tracks." He turned serious. "I saw the demons following you."

Xander stepped forward. "What are you not telling us, boy?"

Ethrang stared at the glowering wizard, and a look of anger crossed his features. "This is why I didn't want to tell you. I knew you would think I was trying to rob you or something. The truth is I heard your speech and felt inspired, so I wanted to...fight for a cause. I was a street kid stealing and selling Wack. I wanted to change, that's all. I thought you were going to Toron, but then I realized after Thundar you were really headed for the Guild. I have magic, so I decided to come." He looked down at his feet.

Chip felt a pang of pity for him. There was something he was not telling them, but everyone had their secrets.

Xander did not seem convinced. "How did you arrive at the Guild before us?"

"I didn't. I came right after you. The gates were still open."

The old wizard studied him. Chip could tell he was unsure.

Xander seemed to think about something then changed his demeanour. "Very well. Enough questions, young man. Do not be shy if you need to tell us anything important in the future. Are you going to watch any of the tournaments?"

Ethrang grinned. "I am not shy. I have already challenged someone to a duel today. He tried to bully me, so I did what you did. He wouldn't play fisticuffs with me for some reason but agreed to duel. I will battle him later today. Come if you want. I'm going to watch the Protectors for a bit. Talk to you later." They nodded, and he hurried away.

"He is withholding something," Xander said. Mina and Siz strolled up.

"I think he is alright. Remember, Ethrang is an orphan from

Banfar, so he's been through a lot. Let's cut him some slack," Chip said.

"He's funny," Mina said, overhearing, watching the skinny boy leave. "And oddly good-looking."

Siz looked at her in shock. "Huh. I don't like him. He probably bullies people and has done mean things. He's an orphan from Banfar. What do you expect?" He spat on the ground, giving the retreating figure a dark look.

Chip was surprised at both of their reactions. "Look, the truth is all of us are a little bit like outcasts if you think about it. Even the queen did not have a 'normal' upbringing. I believe everyone should be given a second chance." Mina had a dreamy look on her face, eyes still on Ethrang as he hurried away, which made Eleanor smile. Siz looked like he was about to throw up.

Xander shook his head in amusement and motioned for Chip to step away from the others. The rest of them got the hint and moved to the side. "Balor and I are going through the histories to see if there are any clues as to the whereabouts of the Light Elves. We must leave the Guild to retrieve the Orb as soon as we find out. Assuming we can find the elves and that King Luminor still has it."

"Well, that is one king we need to find according to the Galad Prophecy and the Assessor's Telling. Who are the other two kings?" Chip asked.

"Dominor is likely the second, and the third could be the Red-Eyed King, though I am not sure. In truth, we do not even know if he is a king."

"How long will it take to go over the histories?"

The wizard gave him a look. "There are countless tomes. It will take some time." Chip looked frustrated. Xander acknowledged his discomfort. "I know our time is limited. The demon army will reach Calgar in the next few days. The good news is we sent a sizable force of Guild members there who will be instrumental in mounting a reasonable defence. In the meantime, we need to find the Light Elves. The prophecies point to us finding them. Skylar is convinced the answer is buried in the histories. In the meantime, take the Trials and get Certified so you can call yourself a wizard." Chip's eyes widened. "You have nothing else to do."

He patted his shoulder and walked away.

Chip sighed and decided to get more information about the First Trial. The section was at the other end of the huge courtyard, opposite the Fifth Trial pavilion. He signalled to the others. "Anyone care to check out the First Trial?" They all nodded and started walking with him.

The boy marvelled at the four immense thousand-foot statues surrounding the Guild. They looked stunning in the morning sun, pointing to the heavens. He glanced down at his robes. They were a luxurious velvet red. He felt self-conscious because he was the only one in the Guild wearing that colour. Behind them, he noticed a fair-sized crowd following. Chip rolled his eyes. Eleanor laughed and took his hand.

"How do you think I have felt my whole life? Don't worry, you will get used to it." She smiled.

"My whole life, I was a nobody," he answered. "Now that I am somebody, it is not what I expected." He remembered thinking the same thing in Banfar. Chip laughed at the irony of it all. A saying from the weapons master popped into his head. "Nothing is easy for anyone. It is all relative. A child who breaks a toy is like a king who drops his crown." The orphan was taught they both feel the same thing. Most people would give much to become famous or hold a position of power, but they do not consider the lack of privacy and the added responsibility.

Chip looked down at his new red cloak and realized again how unique he was. He should not blame anyone for gawking. The boy would likely do the same in their position. He could help so many people. It was a gift, and he would look at it that way.

They arrived at a fenced-off area for the First Trial. A large, older woman with glasses, dressed in yellow robes with white cuffs, sat in a chair with a notepad, explaining something to a student. A large rectangular piece of stone sat in a white chalk circle in the center of the fenced area. It stood almost shoulder height and was at least ten feet long by four feet wide.

"How far do I have to move it?" the student asked. She was a small girl with blond hair wearing yellow robes.

The large woman lowered her glasses. "At the Yellow Level, you only have to push it over on its side, sweetie." The girl nodded solemnly, and her eyes lit a weak yellow. She looked at the stone as if it were her worst enemy. She concentrated, face scrunching, and lifted both hands. The rock trembled, and one side slowly lifted. The girl strained harder, grinding her teeth, until the rock turned just enough to stand on its edge and finally fell over on its side. The girl dropped her hands, exhaling explosively, and smiled with pride. The older woman checked something off and then handed her a paper. The young girl took the slip and held it aloft to read it. Chip could make out "Trial 1 – PASS." The girl squealed with delight before dashing away.

The tester looked at their group, noticing Chip's robes but not saying anything. "Who's next?"

Mina raised her hand and walked forward. "I will go."

The woman looked at her above thick glasses. "I am Yellow Wing Leader Magda, sweetie. Brown Level is much more difficult. You need to lift the rock and place it in the other circle fifty feet yonder then bring it back."

Mina's eyes widened, but she nodded, seizing her Power. She turned her palms upwards and raised them. The rock immediately lifted off the ground, and she guided it to the circle, placing it down for a moment.

"You have only a short while to bring it back," the plump tester said and flipped over an hourglass on the desk in front of her. The small dark-haired girl did not wait and lifted the stone again, returning it to its original position. Mina exhaled and smiled.

Wing Leader Magda nodded. "Well done. This First Trial should be fairly easy for most students. If not, you may have trouble in the other Trials." She looked towards the small blonde girl in yellow robes walking in the distance. "She may not pass the other Trials, I'm afraid, poor thing. It breaks my heart when I see that. She will be barred."

"That's not fair," Eleanor said from the front of the line. "There is no reason that girl should be stripped of her Power because she is not strong enough."

"Life is not fair, Queen of Vanalon." Eleanor looked surprised that she knew her name. "You, of all people, should know. That little girl could form a small yellow dagger with her Power and kill the strongest man in the world. Do not think she is weak. All magic must be controlled. Failing the Trials means the student is not in control or not strong enough to control herself and is, therefore, a danger to all humans. It is not fair, but it is the way. Come forward if you wish to take the Trial." She handed Mina a pass paper. The small girl smiled and moved aside.

The queen stepped forward, still looking unhappy with the explanation. Chip noticed the crowd behind him continuing to grow.

"Place the rock in the circle, I assume?" she asked Magda. It was obvious she wanted to channel her anger.

"No. You have red around your cuffs. I have never seen that before, but I trust the Assessor. I will put you at the Blue Level requirement to compensate. Lift the rock to the height of the Guild wall, then place it in the other circle and bring it back." The queen looked at her in surprise. The Guild wall was two hundred feet high. She looked up then shrugged and seized her Power. Her eyes blazed with a ferocious brown but now had red flecks throughout. Magda's eyes widened.

The rock flew off the ground, then rose higher and higher into the air. Chip could hear gasps from the crowd behind him at the display of raw Power. The huge rock crested the height of the wall and then sank into the other circle fifty feet away. Eleanor paused a moment then lifted her hands again. The rock rose to the wall height before returning to land in front of them with a thump. She released her Power and smiled despite herself. The crowd applauded.

"Very well, indeed." Magda beamed. "You did that better than the

Blues I've seen. You must have been training for a long time on your own."

Eleanor shook her head. "Not really."

"Oh my," Magda said, handing her the slip of paper with a "PASS" on it. She glanced around. "Next."

Siz looked like he was going to throw up. "You go first," he said to Chip.

"Fine," he whispered back to him. "But try to relax."

The Guardian stepped forward, and the crowd behind him started murmuring. Magda looked him up and down. "My oh my, the Red Level." She lowered her glasses. "I never thought I would live to see the day. I should take prophecy more seriously." She turned and looked at the rock. "What on Earth would a Red Level need to pass?"

She began muttering to herself and then scribbled some calculations on her notepad. She paused and cursed under her breath, scratching out what she had written. The crowd went silent, wondering what she was going to do. Magda frantically scribbled, finally putting what looked like a period on the paper.

"Aha, I've got it!" She looked at him triumphantly. "Raise the rock to the tip of the finger of the nearest statue, then back down into the circle."

It took a moment for the crowd to digest this, causing most students to gasp. Everyone craned their necks to look up at the statue, which was the yellow-robed woman a thousand feet tall. It was five times the height of the wall.

Magda smiled brightly and showed him the paper. After all that scribbling, Chip had expected to see a mathematical formula with all kinds of numbers, but instead, it was a simple outline of the female wizard statue with a tiny dot at the tip of her finger. His eyes widened, which caused her to nod with pride as if she had invented a brilliant new test. He heard a giggle behind him.

Turning, Chip saw Ethrang in his green robe leaning over him, looking at the picture. The blond orphan boy laughed aloud and slapped him on the shoulder.

"Piece of cake, Guardian." His laughter was infectious, and others in the crowd began to chuckle, realizing the impossibility of the task. Chip knew no wizard had likely ever tried such a feat. The Power diminished with distance, and the finger's tip looked a long way away.

As if reading his mind, Magda said, "No one has ever done that." She smiled and turned to the crowd. "Please back up, everybody. You will be crushed if he loses control on the way down." She shooed them away, then lifted her chair and walked to the edge of the fence before sitting back down, ensuring she was safe. "Anytime you are ready," she called distantly.

Chip looked at Eleanor, who was trying not to laugh. Ethrang was whispering something to Mina, causing her to double over. Siz had a mixture of disgust, fear, and fascination on his face. The crowd moved back, and some students shook their heads as if there was no way anyone could pass such a test. Chip took a deep breath in and breathed slowly out. He thought of the queen in pain and broke through his Wall. He had already expended magic against the Demon King and considered waiting a day. Then again it would be an interesting test.

Chip pulled in his Power, eyes blazing a fiery red. He vaguely noticed Magda cover her mouth in surprise. Separating his hands, he seized the rock on both sides and raised his arms. The stone shot upwards, easily passing over the top of the wall. It only took moments for it to reach halfway up the statue.

After a while, it began to slow, and he fed his Power into the bottom, pushing it higher. He was aware of how distance made it harder. He pulled in more Power and continued feeding it magic, concentrating on the rock, which now looked the size of a pebble. Shouts of wonder began to erupt behind him.

"He's getting closer."

"Look how small the rock is now."

"He's not going to make it!"

The rock reached the statue's head, over nine hundred feet in the air. He gave it a last push, concentrating on the small dot. It sailed up the outstretched arm and along the finger before briefly resting on the very tip. He began to strain as he almost lost sight of it. The crowd started clapping. He pulled the rock off the tip and let it fall in a controlled manner.

Suddenly, everyone heard a distant crack, then a loud grind. Above the falling rock, to Chip's horror, the statue's finger cracked at its base and began falling down with the tiny rock. Worse, it was directly over the crowd. The stone finger was at least five times the size of the rock and much thicker. The boy felt a wave of weariness and fear. He knew he had to make an instant decision. Chip abandoned the rock, letting it fall, and with both hands raised, he sent his magic into the finger, stopping its descent. With a grunt, he pushed up on the appendage with a large expenditure of magic, resetting it on the hand. The rectangular rock was hurtling down at frightening speed towards the crowd.

For a mad moment, he realized that if it struck the queen, the prophecy would come true. It would be his fault. Using both hands, he stabilized the finger, channelling Power into the base, melding it to the stone palm, ignoring the hurtling missile that was getting larger at an alarming rate. Finally, he let go, satisfied that the appendage was stable. He was out of time. With the rock just above them, Chip flung a huge cushion of Power under it, causing its descent to slow then stop at the last moment, directly above the crowd. The students started breathing again, realizing they were all holding their breaths.

Ethrang jumped up and slapped it, laughing. Chip moved the rock back to its starting point, trembling with fatigue, and placed it down. The crowd went berserk.

"Hail the Guardian!" Ethrang shouted. The students joined in the cheer. Chip wiped beads of sweat off his brow and took a bow. Magda rushed towards him, carrying her chair. She sat down in her old spot and with a beaming face handed him a piece of paper.

"It's a pass! If you had killed any students, I would have switched it to a fail. Next!" she called, looking around.

"I will go," Ethrang said, leaping ahead of Siz to the front of the line.

Magda looked at him. "The Green Level test is to raise the rock my height off the ground twice..."

Even as she said it, the blond boy's eyes blazed a shockingly bright green with a silver tinge, and the rock lifted up and down ten feet twice. He held out his hand, grinning. She looked at him sternly, then sighed and scribbled out a note. Siz stared at Ethrang with a strange expression, likely jealous of the boy's confidence.

"Next time, let me finish speaking, young man," Magda scolded him. "If I had known your attitude, I would have made it more difficult." She handed him a pass. Ethrang held it up for the other students to see. "Next!"

Everyone looked at Siz, who had not gone yet. He was still staring at the green-robed boy then noticed the crowd behind him and shook his head. "Another time," he said, "way too many people." The others were going to protest, but after seeing his consternation, they decided to let him be.

"Come watch your friend in the Protector's Arena," Ethrang blurted to Chip. "Chase is doing his Final Test soon. He cannot fight in the tournament unless he passes." The skinny boy started walking, waving them on. Chip and the others followed, wanting to know what the Protector test would entail. He had always envisioned himself as a soldier, given his training with the weapons master. He realized how much his world had changed in such a brief time.

They followed the fast-moving blond orphan. The students in the crowd parted, many congratulating Chip on his impressive feat with the stone. He nodded in thanks, which put smiles on their faces. He was beginning to enjoy the higher status and adoration, realizing it allowed him to elevate another person's well-being. As they walked, the boy noticed a huge crowd gathering in the yard around the arena. He felt a sense of relief that, for once, he was not the center of attention. Then he realized his best friend was taking the ultimate test, and his heart rate increased. As the group approached the spectacle, they could feel a palpable energy surrounding the event. Something big was about to happen.

8

They reached the arena to see Chase standing in the center alone. The Protectors stood off to one side behind a railing. Students and staff filled the seats to capacity. It seemed word had spread regarding the reputation of Xander's "Invincible Protector." Balor himself sat front and center, watching everything. Xander was beside him with Garth to his right.

Maxim, the High Wizard's personal Protector and master trainer, stood in the arena before Chase, speaking in a loud voice. "The Final Test is composed of five challenges. You must pass them all. You will be given up to one hour. The hourglass will be turned when the test commences. The current record is twenty-nine minutes. You will be healed, if necessary, between each round." He gestured at a group of Yellow Level wizard healers standing beside the Protectors. "If another combatant strikes a mortal blow or knocks you unconscious, you will be deemed to have failed the Final Test. Those who fail will be escorted from the Guild. State your trainer's name."

"Garth Stone, the weapons master," Chase said proudly, suppressing a grin that did not go unnoticed. The other Protectors nodded in respect, and the students watching whispered excitedly.

Maxim's star student, Carvor, glowered. Garth, seated behind the rail, remained impassive.

"The first challenge is to last one minute with three Protectors of your choosing. You will have no weapons. You must remain conscious at the end. Choose," Maxim instructed.

Chase looked at the Protectors gathered in the waiting area on his right side. Many had looks of anticipation on their faces. Some showed downright contempt. "Any volunteers?" Chase asked with a smile, eyes glinting with red chips. All the Protectors raised their hands. "I'll tell you what," he said, turning to Maxim, "you choose the three best from amongst yourselves and send them in. Bring some healers too, would you?"

Maxim showed a brief flash of anger then turned to the Protectors. "Carvor, Hunter, and Sheldor step forward. I choose them per the trainee's request."

Carvor stepped forward nimbly, muscles rippling, walking like a tiger. Hunter came next, thin but ripped, moving quickly, eyes calculating. Sheldor came last, a massive Protector with huge arms and chest. He strode forward with legs like tree trunks. Chip's eyes widened, as did most of the crowds'.

It seemed impossible that anyone could survive a beating from those three for a full minute. They surrounded Chase, who now looked relatively small in comparison. Three healers took positions around the combatants at a safe distance. Maxim had a faint, self-satisfied smile on his face. Chase noticed Chip and winked at him. The Guardian could not help but grin.

The gesture did not escape Maxim's notice. "Begin," he shouted.

Hunter leapt in with a jumping front kick aimed at Chase's chest. At the same time, Sheldor ran forward to tackle him. Carvor came from behind with a savage right hook. It looked like there was nowhere to go for a split second, then Chase moved blindingly fast. He grabbed Hunter's front foot and pulled him forward, ducking simultaneously. Carvor's fist met air where Chase's head had just been and instead connected with Hunter's jaw full force. Sheldor ended up tackling both of his companions at the same time, which caused all three to end up in a heap. Chase stood to the side, unscathed. The crowd sat wide-eyed.

Carvor and Sheldor leapt to their feet, but Hunter remained unconscious on his back. His chin was crushed inward. Chase put his front foot forward, awaiting the next attack. Sheldor moved to his right side while Carvor took his left.

Again, they attacked at the same time, which made sense. The huge Protector swung his hammer fist at the tall boy's head while Carvor opted to go low, trying to sweep his legs with a kick. Chase waited motionless, watching them both commit to their attacks, then leapt straight in the air and kicked out sideways, his foot connecting with a loud crack on Sheldor's nose.

The big man's attempted right hook stopped short, and he recoiled in pain as his nose disappeared into his face. Carvor's leg met air, and he sprang backwards. Sheldor clutched his face, exposing his midsection.

Without waiting, Chase spun and gave a full-force turning kick with his left foot into the big man's ribs. There was a loud crack that the entire arena could hear, and the Protector fell to his knees, grunting. Chase, keeping an eye on Carvor, back-kicked Sheldor directly in the face, sending him flying onto his back, unmoving. Carvor's expression betrayed a hint of surprise then steely determination. Chase stood up and circled him, carefully keeping his left foot forward. The crowd had gone silent, many with faces in complete shock. Even the other Protectors were looking at each other apprehensively.

Carvor leapt in lightning-fast with a jab, followed by a front kick. Chase expertly blocked both. Maxim's star pupil danced in and out, throwing a flurry of kicks and punches, all blocked. In frustration, knowing time was running out, Carvor executed a jumping knee. It was the mistake Chase was looking for.

With stunning speed, he kicked straight up, the sole of his foot connecting underneath the front of Carvor's knee, causing the Protector to somersault in a full circle. As his head came around, Chase executed a downward elbow strike on the base of his skull, knocking him out. Carvor's face struck the dirt floor hard, not moving. Chip had never seen Chase move with such speed and strength.

All three combatants were unconscious around him.

"Time," called Maxim, trying to hide his irritation. "Healers."

The Yellow wizards rushed in, waving for extra support. Six more healers entered from the side, and groups of three surrounded each downed combatant. Shortly afterwards, they were all standing. Carvor's red face was still covered in dirt, which he tried to wipe away angrily. Hunter looked like he was asking the others what happened. Sheldor gave Chase a respectful nod as they all moved off to the side.

"You have passed the first challenge." The crowd, silent and shocked until now, erupted in applause. Maxim glowered and raised his hand. "The second challenge is to run from one railing to the other. There will be four Protectors in your way. You have five minutes to reach the other side. If they take you to the ground and force you to submit, you must start over. You can only use wrestling moves, no striking. Choose your four."

"Again, it's your choice," Chase said calmly.

"You will address me as master trainer," Maxim corrected. "Any volunteers?" This time, only about half the Protectors raised their hands. The others were looking elsewhere. He pointed to four combatants, one at a time.

They ducked under the railing and took positions in the center of the field. Those chosen were shorter, stockier than the others, and better built for wrestling. Chase started with his hand on the rail nearest the Protectors. The looks he received from those watching were ones of anger, fear, and growing respect. Carvor had a menacing look, angry he was not chosen for this event.

"Begin," barked Maxim. Chase ran at a light jog towards the center. Chip knew he was weighing his options. It would be difficult to evade four trained Protectors in great physical condition. They converged on his position, holding their hands out before them and squatting low to the ground. At the last second, Chase dodged left, gambling with a front roll to escape his first attacker.

This worked to evade the Protector in front, but the second man pivoted and wrapped his arm around the tall boy's stomach. Chase did a full spin, windmilling his arms, and escaped the second man. By then, the third stocky Protector had leapt at him like a projectile. He seized the tall boy in a vice-like body grip, giving him no choice but to roll with it. The man's goal was to land on top of him, which Chase allowed for a split second before turning into the direction of momentum, which carried the Protector overtop him.

He slid out between the man's legs, seeing the open field ahead. It seemed too easy, so he instinctively rolled to his right, which avoided the fourth combatant trying to dive on him. Chase sprang forward three steps, glancing at the original attacker now converging on him from an angle.

At the last moment, he paused, hooked the man's elbow, and viciously spun him forward, where he face-planted into the dirt. Chase turned and sprinted, seeing the other three converging again. They had more momentum, so he turned to the man on the right just as they reached him and grabbed his shirt. Chase fell on his own back and twisted, throwing the Protector over himself straight into the other two. He heard some bones crack, and all three went down.

Chase rolled to his feet and turned with only a few steps to go. He knew the fourth attacker was almost upon him again, so before he reached the railing, the tall boy planted both feet and somersaulted backwards over the man, grabbing the back of his shirt and yanking him down hard. He risked a glance at the others, who were still in a pile holding various body parts and then sauntered to the railing. He touched it to tumultuous cheers from the crowd.

"Healers!" Maxim called between clenched teeth. Again, the Yellow wizards ran out to heal the Protectors. The most severe injury was a broken rib followed by a fractured wrist. "Do you wish a rest?" he asked. Chase shook his head.

"You have passed the second challenge. The third challenge is the sword." Maxim tried to hide his smile. "Would you like me to pick this one, too?"

"Sure," Chase said offhandedly. Chip shook his head. It was obvious he was being baited.

"Then I will nominate my finest swordsman," Maxim said. Carvor began stepping forward proudly.

"Me." The Silver Sword Champion stopped in shock as everyone gasped.

Maxim stepped forward and drew his own sword, smiling in satisfaction. There seemed to be a flurry of activity next to the High Wizard as the cleric grabbed a book and began rifling through it. A Protector off to the side threw Chase a sword, which was a basic one.

Garth Stone then stood up and drew his sword in one smooth motion. Maxim paused, turning to look at him with narrowed eyes. With an expert twist of his hand, Garth flipped his sword, grasping its tip, and threw it at the master trainer with deadly force. Maxim did not move but watched as the sword passed inches from his shoulder to land between the feet of Garth's pupil.

Chase smiled, throwing away the basic sword, and reached down to grasp the hilt of his teacher's blade. The crowd looked back and forth, feeling different emotions at every turn. The air was electric. Carvor stepped back, realizing what was going on, and smiled.

Maxim turned and advanced towards Chase. He stopped ten feet from the tall boy, standing straight, and lifted his sword so the tip was at eye level.

"You must score three points to win. None can be a full death blow. Healers will stand at the ready." Even as he said it, three Yellow wizards ran to stand a distance behind them. "Begin!" he yelled, leaping forward with incredible speed, the tip of his sword barely touching Chase's stomach.

"Point!" yelled Maxim. He then held up his hand and turned to the Protectors, who huddled in a circle.

"Concur," they said in agreement, indicating the point was valid. Chase looked down at his stomach and shook his head. He was clearly angry that he had been caught off guard.

"Begin," the master trainer shouted again, leaping forward. This time, Chase was ready. He parried then flicked his sword up at the man's throat. Maxim blocked it in a blur of motion as he stepped back, then started circling. His moves were fluid and concise, dangerously quick.

He came at the boy from many different angles, dancing in and out with expert precision. Chase parried and countered each time, but the man always seemed to anticipate his response. The tall boy changed his strategy and unleashed a blistering flurry of strokes at Maxim, who was forced to back up.

The older man parried furiously and then, looking overwhelmed, turned to run. Chase leapt in to drive his weapon between the man's exposed shoulders, but Maxim dropped to the ground, his sword point coming back up between his elbow and ribs, driving straight into the boy's heart. Chase grimaced, leaping back, anger crossing his face at his stupidity. Maxim turned and stared at the boy's chest in shock, anticipating deep wounds but realizing only his shirt was torn.

"Point," he called, still looking with disbelief at the lack of injury. It should have been close to a death blow. The other Protectors conferred again. "Concur," they said after only a moment's deliberation.

Maxim nodded, then stood straight again, holding his sword aloft. "Two points to zero. Begin!" A smile now covered his face. Chip could see in the master trainer's face that he knew he was a better swordsman. He only had to finish the trainee off. He wanted Chase to fail and be ejected from the Guild, and then he would likely deal with Garth, rectifying old wounds.

Chase stepped back, letting his anger settle while he circled the man. Chip could tell he was going through all their training tactics in his mind, deciding which one would work, looking for a weakness. Maxim jumped in to strike then leapt back to parry. His form was perfect. The weapons master taught them that everyone had a weakness, even if it was not apparent. You just had to find it.

Again, the older man leapt in and attacked then stepped back. Something was not right. He leapt again. There! Chip could see it. Chase noticed his best friend's reaction from the railing and continued to study the man intently. They traded blows. The tall boy did not see it yet, but he at least knew there was a weakness. Two attacks later, Chase stepped back and smiled, figuring it out. Maxim looked at him warily, and they circled again. The master trainer looked low then at the last instant struck high at the boy's face.

Chase ducked, striking low. His sword went several inches into the older man's stomach. It was a risk because if he had guessed wrong, the Invincible Protector could have been skewered.

"Point," Chase shouted. The Protectors turned to confer. Carvor looked angry. Given the wet pool of blood forming in the older man's shirt, it took way too long for them to deliberate.

"Concur," they finally agreed, unable to ignore the obvious wound. The crowd clapped excitedly. Healers rushed over, and Chip felt the familiar crackle of magic. After a few moments, they stepped back, and Maxim appeared healed.

"Two points to one. Begin," the master trainer said through clenched teeth and started circling. He executed a blistering barrage at Chase, venting his rage. The boy parried with precision and counterattacked. The older man looked like he was having trouble and leapt to the side to escape. Chase went after him with an overhand strike then changed his mind mid-swing and leapt back instead. He was lucky he did, as Maxim had been baiting him.

Seeing that his gambit did not pay off, Maxim resumed his dance in and out. It was the third attack that Chase took advantage of. He waited for the master trainer to look high just before striking low, and at the same time, the boy whipped his sword across the man's neck, all the while concaving his stomach to avoid the thrust. It was a huge risk, but again it paid off. He was getting better at reading the man's bluff by attacking exactly where he looked at first, which was the opposite of his intended attack. Maxim stumbled back, clutching his throat, blood spurting between his fingers.

"Healers!" Chase called with a look of concern. They rushed forward, surrounding the older man. He fell to the ground, gurgling. After a minute, one healer stood up with a look of anguish, calling for more help. The rest of the Yellow wizards ran over as the man's body began convulsing. Garth stood up with concern. Chip ducked under the railing and ran to the man's side. Maxim's face was purple. He was clearly dying. Blood had filled his lungs, so he was unable to breathe. The boy seized the older man's shoulder and grabbed the hand of one of the Yellow Healers. He broke through his Wall, sensed the link, and then wrenched their Power to his will. He had no time to explain himself. The man had moments left to live. The boy vaporized the blood in his lungs and forced fresh air into his chest. It was not enough. Maxim's heart stopped beating as the air filled him. The Yellow wizards cried out in frustration.

Chip instinctively compressed the man's heart repeatedly, forcing his blood to move. At the same time, he inflated his lungs, spreading life-giving air throughout his body. The boy sent his magic throughout Maxim, searching for further injury. He noticed his throat hole was fixed, but the inner tube had not been repaired properly. Blood still leaked into his lungs. He healed the hole by reconnecting the flesh and searched for other damage. The man's body was intact, so he decided to scan his head. There was blood in the back of his brain, likely caused by his fall to the ground. Nobody had checked that part. Chip dissolved the blood, allowing his brain to settle, then reconnected the tiny vessel that had burst. Maxim's eyes opened. He sucked in a deep breath and sat up.

"Get off me!" he yelled, backhanding Chip across the mouth. The Guardian stood up in his red robes, eyes blazing with rage. He released the linked Yellows, who fell over from exhaustion. He pointed at Maxim, feeling an almost uncontrollable fury. The boy floated him in the air, daring him to attack. The master trainer looked deep into his blazing eyes and finally showed fear.

"My apologies, Guardian," he said, trying to bow. "I overreacted."

Chip set him down. "You are a Protector and a master trainer. Act like one. Chase has fought with honour. Treat him fairly." The Guardian turned and walked away, releasing his Power. There was another moment of silence.

"Point?" Chase said awkwardly.

Maxim did not even turn to the Protectors. "They concur. It is tied at two points each…"

"Excuse me?" Everyone stopped. The master trainer turned in annoyance. The cleric was standing at the rail with a book in his hand. "Sorry to bother you, but I am afraid this sword challenge has not been sanctioned."

"What do you mean, cleric?" Maxim asked acidly.

"The Book of Rules for the Final Test says that the sword challenge must be between an apprentice and a Protector. Trainers, teachers, and testers may not participate. In addition, the challenger must be another apprentice or student who has been a Protector for less than two years. I assume this rule stops an apprentice from being challenged by a master, which would be unfair. It is unlikely anyone would pass the challenge unless they were better than the master, which makes no sense, as they would then become the master. The point is it is against the rules." The cleric looked up. Maxim studied him as if he were a cockroach, then looked around at the crowd.

"I set the rules here. It is my Final Test…" the master trainer began.

"Ahem." The sound of the person clearing his throat was unmistakable. High Wizard Balor stood up with an icy look.

"I set the rules as I am High Wizard of the Guild. I have had no reason to stray from this book, which has been the official Protector Final Test for over three thousand years. You will heed the cleric and choose another combatant." Balor sat down.

"Of course, High Wizard. Forgive my audacity." Maxim gave Chase a withering look and turned to the group of Protectors to select another.

Before he could speak, Balor stood up again. "Oh, and I recommend not choosing Carvor. It would ruin the excitement of them meeting in the finals in the upcoming Silver Sword."

Maxim showed dismay but bowed again. "Of course, High Wizard. I choose Hunter."

The other Protectors gave Hunter a wide berth and shook their heads as if they felt sorry for him. He displayed a momentary look of consternation and then walked forward. Maxim gave the man his sword and walked away, back stiff.

"We will start the third challenge again. Square up, combatants. Begin," Maxim said without emotion.

Chase waited for the man to strike. Hunter feinted several times then leapt in. As soon as he did, the boy struck blazingly quick, slicing across his stomach and holding the tip of his sword to Hunter's throat.

"Point," he said, withdrawing his sword. Hunter gulped.

There was a quick concur, and it was one point to nothing for Chase. Healers rushed in to repair the gash, and the bout continued. The following two points lasted mere moments with similar results. Hunter turned and walked away, too embarrassed to be healed.

Maxim looked glum. "You have passed the third challenge. The fourth challenge involves any weapon of your choice other than a sword. You will face two combatants. You must incapacitate them or strip them of their weapons. If you drop your weapon or are too injured to continue, you lose. Do you wish to choose?" Chase gestured for the man to pick. Maxim smiled with relief and looked at the Protectors. "Any volunteers?" This time, nobody raised their hands. Some were even looking at the ground as if studying the soil.

"Sheldor and Bulch, step forward," Maxim ordered. The big man from the first challenge sighed, then flexed his massive muscles, ducking under the railing.

Chase nodded, expecting the selection, then stared wide-eyed as Bulch stood up. He had been hidden the whole time because the giant was sitting down. The man was easily seven feet tall with heavily muscled arms and legs so long it made him walk funny. His face looked deformed, with tufts of hair sprouting in odd spots. His two bloodshot eyes were impossibly far apart, and the man's teeth had been filed to sharp points. He even carried a club!

Chase looked at Maxim, who was grinning deviously. Chip realized this was their rabbit in the hat. His best friend groaned and waited while the two approached. Sheldor looked like Bulch's child.

"Choose your weapon," Maxim instructed Chase. The tall boy turned to see a variety of clubs, daggers, maces, and axes, among other implements, along the back railing. He had been trained in all of them but needed to decide which would work best against these monstrosities. Chip watched him consider the axe, but Bulch's limbs were so huge it might get stuck in them. Daggers would also be useless, as they would not reach deep enough into the giant man's body parts. Sheldor chose a mace, which made Chase roll his eyes. He ended up deciding on a club, the same as Bulch. The crowd went silent as they watched with bated breath. The two men faced the boy, who now looked diminutive, even comical.

"Begin!" the master trainer said with satisfaction.

Bulch immediately moved sideways like a crab, much faster than a person that size should be able to. Sheldor ran straight at him, swinging his mace savagely. Chase sprung into action, sliding through the gap the two huge men left before it closed. The mace went over his head as the tall boy swung down hard on Sheldor's right knee with all his strength. There was a loud crack, and the man screamed.

As he fell, Bulch's club appeared where Sheldor had stood, swinging across unimpeded, catching Chase by surprise. It struck him hard in the shoulder, sending him cartwheeling across the ground. Bulch ran at him with a wide, spider-like gait as if he had ridden a horse too long. His speed was remarkable, and he reached Chase before he could get up. At the last moment, the tall boy saw the massive club coming straight down to crush his chest. He rolled to the right, and it slammed into the ground, spraying up a cloud of dirt.

Chip realized that, despite Chase's newfound strength, Bulch could end his friend if he struck him right. The boy leapt to his feet then ducked, correctly anticipating Sheldor's mace whistling through the air at his head. Chase back kicked him in the stomach then spun around, swinging his club in a wide arc, striking the man across the face. Teeth and blood flew sideways, and Sheldor dropped to his knees. That was all the time Chase had as Bulch was upon him, using both hands to bring the oversized club straight down on the top of his head.

The boy brought his undersized club around in time to block the attack, and everyone heard a loud snap as it broke in two. The larger club went through and struck Chase's head. He staggered and looked dizzily at the stump of the club in his right hand as blood poured down his face. Bulch grinned madly, transferring his oversized weapon to his other hand.

Chip had never seen Chase ever get really mad. Regardless of the circumstances, his friend always had a joke or a quip ready. He lived a happy-go-lucky life and took all challenges in stride, usually finding humour in everything.

Now, his friend stood in front of this seven-foot monster, blood dripping down his face, and he looked angry. The red chips in his blue eyes seemed to shine brighter. In a blur of motion, he leapt first onto Sheldor, who was still on his knees and seized the handle of his mace. With his other hand, he bashed him across the head with the stump of his club, knocking him senseless.

With the mace in one hand and the broken club in the other, he turned back to face Bulch. The huge man paused, seeing his anger, and for the first time showed a hint of doubt. Then he bellowed and ran at the boy.

Chase's hands and feet moved at the same time, all with frightening speed. He ducked low and swung the club stump into Bulch's ribs, then slammed the mace into the huge man's front foot, stopping his motion and causing him to grunt. The boy moved around the monster without slowing, striking him from every angle with mace and wood.

The giant tried to swing the large club again, but the tall boy struck the hand holding it until it turned purple and broke apart in a mixture of blood and bone fragments. Bulch bellowed again, managing to hold on to the club with his other hand, but now he sounded more like an injured animal than a savage beast.

Chase continued his strikes, moving around him with lightning speed. Each blow created a snap or pop, and bones and bruises formed on sight.

Chip realized that Chase's rage seemed to magnify his skill just as his own anger fueled his magic. The huge man fell to one knee and then to the other as Chase chopped him down. Broken bones stuck out of his body at odd angles. Bulch made one last attempt to swing his club at the boy, but Chase brought the mace down on his wrist and snapped it in two. The club dropped to the ground as Chase swung the butt of his broken club straight up into the man's chin.

The giant's eyes rolled back, and Bulch slowly fell like a falling tree. The sound of him hitting the ground was palpable. Chase stood in the arena, covered in blood, and tossed his weapons to the side.

"Next!" he yelled at Maxim, facing him with hands clenched. The crowd cheered madly.

For a moment, the master trainer was speechless, looking at the boy with disbelief. "Healers," he called weakly.

Every Yellow off to the side ran forward this time, knowing it would take a small army to heal Bulch. Other wizards from the crowd joined in, seeing how exhausted the healers were. Several approached Chase to heal his head wound, but he waved them off and waited for his final challenge.

After a short while, both men got up and walked away with support. Sheldor looked at him with disbelief, shaking his head. Bulch actually grinned and nodded at the boy, his version of showing respect.

Maxim raised his hands for silence. "You have passed the fourth challenge." The applause from the crowd was so deafening that the man had to wait with an irritated expression until it died down. "The fifth and final challenge involves a wizard of your choice from the Yellow or Green levels. Choose any weapons you wish. You must defeat the wizard or fail. Whoever is unconscious, incapacitated, or submits loses. Who do you choose?" Chase waved the question away as before. "Very well, I choose Green Wing Leader Storm." Maxim smiled evilly.

The cleric immediately stood up in the crowd. "Storm is a Blue Level filling in for the real Green Leader Pete, who is returning from a trip to Toron."

"He wears green robes and resides in the Green Wing," Maxim said smoothly. As the book says, he is from the Green Level."

The cleric looked at him. "I think the meaning is clear. 'From' may be the wrong word, but the intent..." He looked at Balor, who shrugged.

"We can debate it at the next council. Storm is Green in all aspects for now and has the authority of the Green Wing Leader. Carry on," the High Wizard intoned. The cleric bowed and sat down.

Maxim smiled. "Storm, do you accept the challenge?"

A middle-aged man with black hair stood up with a flourish, green robes swirling. He had grey hair at his temples and a strong jaw. He carried himself with an aura of power. The wizard walked into the arena and stood before Maxim.

"I accept, master trainer." He turned and faced the boy.

"Excellent," Maxim said to Chase. "Take all the weapons you wish." The tall boy looked at the array of implements. He picked up several daggers, buckled on a sword, slung a shield over his back, put a small axe in his belt, and grabbed a bow and arrows, knocking the first one. Maxim blinked then smiled. This time, he looked confident the boy would have no chance. "Begin!"

With anger still in his eyes, Chase unleashed the first arrow, then ran at an angle, continuing to fire in a blur of motion. Storm immediately erected a blue shield as his eyes blazed to life. The arrows melted into it. Chase continued to unleash the deadly missiles, forcing the man to maintain his protection.

Chip knew his friend could not pierce the shield, but it forced the wizard to expend Power. Eventually, the entire quiver was empty, and he discarded it on the ground. Storm seized the moment, releasing the shield, and pointed his hands at the boy. It was a mistake that Chase had anticipated, for even as he dropped the quiver, a small dagger fired from his other hand. The shield dropped, allowing the knife to fly through the air and plant hilt deep in the man's stomach. He looked down in shock, staggering backwards. The crowd gasped.

Storm gritted his teeth, flinging his hands at Chase, who rolled to the side and threw another dagger. This time the wizard created a new blue shield in time. The boy was much closer now and ran the last few feet to launch himself on the man. Storm held the shield in place, but the impact knocked him off his feet.

Chase ignored the burns from the wizard's magic, which barely seemed to affect him. Instead, he picked the man up and slammed him to the ground. The shield wavered as Storm gasped for air. Chase grabbed the wizard again and slammed him once more. This time, the shield dropped, giving the boy enough time to unhook his axe and bury it deep in the man's shoulder. Storm screamed and out of instinct sent wizard's fire from his good hand into the boy's chest.

Chase grunted as he flew back. His shirt burned off, and his skin smoked, but, if anything, he looked angrier. More fire came at him, yet even as it did, the boy dove and flipped his last dagger expertly, striking the man a second time in the stomach. The fire died out as Storm screamed, clutching his middle. The red chips in Chase's eyes shone as he drew his sword and dived on his opponent, who was now writhing in pain, doing everything he could to get the maniac off him. Bits of wizard fire flew out of his fingers, and a half-formed shield developed as Chase hacked at him, giving him no reprive. More wounds appeared on the man as the sword pierced the openings in his defence. Storm screamed once more, and the shield disappeared. Chase inserted the point of his sword under the wizard's chin and put his face right up to the dying man. Blood covered the tall boy, and the chips in his eyes shone a wicked red.

"Do you concede, Wizard?" Chase asked in a deadly voice.

"I concede," Storm begged. "Please, you win." The boy stared into his eyes for a moment longer then stood up and tossed the sword away. He faced the crowd with no shirt on, his chest smoking, and raised his hands.

The sound that erupted reverberated throughout the Wizard's Guild. Everyone leapt to their feet, even High Wizard Balor, and applauded emphatically. The anger left Chase, and he smiled. Maxim looked at him with shock, then his expression finally changed to one of respect. He nodded to the tall boy.

"You have passed the fifth and final challenge. You have done so admirably, winning over the people, including myself. I confess I did not make it easy. You made your trainer, Garth Stone, proud."

Chip looked over to see something he never thought he would.

The weapons master stood looking at Chase, his eyes wet, and bowed. The applause was deafening. Chip felt a lump in his throat and turned to his best friend, who looked at him at the same time.

After all those years of training and practicing together, they shared a moment, realizing they had achieved something special. Both boys broke out in broad smiles, acknowledging each other as only best friends can.

"I now Certify you as a Protector of the Guild. You will be assigned a wizard to defend to the end of your days," Maxim declared.

Chase raised his hands, commanding silence. The crowd responded respectfully, the noise dying down. "I have already sworn to protect my dearest friend, Chip Oathbinder. I pledge my allegiance to defend him to the end of days."

Maxim paused. Protectors did not choose whom they would protect. He seemed about to rebuke him but turned around and looked at the High Wizard instead.

"This is against protocol," Balor intoned loudly. The crowd went silent. The High Wizard looked at the Guardian standing to the side in his red robes. "However, if ever a Protector deserved a chance to choose, it would be now. Do you, Chip Oathbinder, Guardian of Humanity, accept Chase Longfellow as your... 'Invincible Protector' from now until the end of his days."

Chip turned to the High Wizard. "It would be the greatest honour of my life. I accept."

"So be it," Balor proclaimed. The crowd, unable to stay quiet any longer, exploded with deafening cheers and applause.

"Hail the Guardian, and Hail the Invincible Protector," the crowd shouted, and the sound reverberated for a long time throughout the Guild.

9

After several minutes of extended applause, Maxim raised his hands. The crowd grudgingly quieted. "What is the time for the Final Test?" he asked the timekeeper sitting behind him.

"Thirty minutes."

The crowd sighed then clapped. Chase had almost beaten Garth's record.

"Ahem." The cleric raised his hand. "Excuse me. The duel with our master trainer does not count and must be omitted." The timekeeper thought about it then nodded and scribbled a new calculation on his sheet.

"I stand corrected," the timekeeper said. "The Final Test was completed in twenty-three minutes, a new record." Maxim's jaw dropped. The crowd drank it in, exploding with noise. The other Protectors came out from the side and congratulated Chase. Carvor stalked off with a sour look. The wizard Storm was beside him, glowering. Bulch stood up and parted the group, walking up to Chase. He towered over the boy, who was not short and grinned.

"Good. Bulch thinks you good." The giant man slapped him on the back, nearly knocking him over, and walked away.

Sheldor came up and shook his hand. "I'd fight alongside you any day. It has been an honour. Welcome to the Protectors." Chase thanked him and smiled.

Chip, waiting patiently to the side, stepped in front of his best friend, giving him a heartfelt embrace.

"You actually look like a wizard now," Chase laughed, staring at the boy's red robes.

"Not yet. I have not passed the Trials. You, however, are a Protector," Chip said in awe. "You finally did it. Best thing I ever saw. My goodness, I don't think I could have done much better." He laughed, and they shared a look. Chip seized his Power and dissolved the blood on his friend. He then examined his wounds, ready to heal him, but stopped, pushing his friend to arm's length. "Your wounds," he said in amazement. "You don't have any." Chase blinked then shrugged.

"He is a special lad," said a strong voice behind them. Chip turned to see Balor approach with Xander. Garth followed respectfully to the side. "Somehow, your Power has infused him," the High Wizard inferred. "It occurred when you healed him in the cornfields. Queen Eleanor also reaped the benefit. Your blood mixed with theirs. Skylar and I have discussed it and tried it with our own Protectors with no success. We are missing something that you alone possess. If all our Protectors could benefit from this…unique ability, we would be much more powerful. You are unique, Chip Oathbinder, and so is your Protector.

"We will discuss this further at another time. I look forward to administering your Fifth Trial when you are ready. In the meantime, we are scouring the histories to determine how to find King Luminor and the Light Elves. All prophecy points to those books, but I confess it is like finding a red-eyed baby. Difficult, yet not impossible."

He let out a rare, small smile. "I am pleased with both of your performances so far. You are uniting the Guild behind you, giving them purpose and strength. Wars cannot be won by the faint-hearted. Utter conviction and belief in each other are paramount to our success. We need an army such as the world has never seen to stand a chance."

He turned to Chase and put a hand on his shoulder. "You have been trained well and put on a good show. I admit it was not entirely fair, but neither is life. Besides, I wanted to see your skills, given your special abilities. I am impressed."

He turned and walked away. Maxim stood at a distance, acknowledged the two boys with a slight nod, and followed the High Wizard. The cleric, trailing both, winked at them and hurried after.

Garth strode up to Chase, standing before his student. "It is rare for an apprentice to eclipse his master so soon." Chase tried to object, but the weapons master raised his hand. "You indeed have newfound enhanced abilities, yet your victories came from here." He tapped the boy's chest. "We can train our bodies, but our minds and hearts matter most. As Protectors, we do not give up. There is always a way, no matter the odds. Well done." He proudly embraced the tall boy and then stepped back, displaying a rare smile.

"My goodness. Not a bad showing." Xander rested his hand on Chase's shoulder. "I thought the poor cleric was going to have a heart attack with all the rule-bending." He bent forward and whispered, "My brother could have intervened, especially at the end, but he likes that sort of thing. It gave him a chance to see your abilities. He always tries to figure out how to improve all Protectors, especially Maxim. He wants an army of almost indestructible soldiers. I do not disagree. I am uncertain though if what you have can be transferable. I suspect there must be a stronger connection than blood, or a matter of life and death has to be involved. We shall see. You two should rest up. Even though it's only midday, you both expended considerable energy."

Chase looked perplexed. "I am fine. I heal fast now. In fact, I am ready for the Silver Sword tournament. I would have done better today, but points were awarded for a simple touch with the tip of the sword, which in a real duel would do little damage."

"I agree," Garth said, "However, we cannot exactly impale an opponent by striking a killing blow. The healers need to get there in time. That is why a strike straight to the heart is forbidden, as are the eyes. You learned much fighting Maxim, as did I. You remembered to always look for a weakness. In rare cases where none are found, remember that any thrust by its very nature has an accompanying weakness. If you strike high, you automatically open your low side, and vice versa. This is a harder weakness to exploit, as it is obvious and easy to defend, but it is there nonetheless. All combatants will also, at some point, tire and reveal a weakness based on the human need to conserve energy. Awareness of this need can stave it off, but eventually, even the greatest will succumb.

"Patience with a skilled opponent is rewarded. Maxim made the same two mistakes based on emotion. He felt you were not a worthy opponent and bluffed his thrust twice, looking opposite where his strike would land. He overused it because it worked the first time. He did not adjust, especially after you exposed it. Maxim allowed his emotions to best him, feeling you were unworthy of corrections. He will not make that mistake again. I look forward to duelling him and expanding my expertise."

They all nodded in appreciation. His analysis of the situation, as usual, was spot on.

"Are you entering the Wizard's Tournament?" Garth asked Chip.

"I do not wish to. In honesty, I think it would be unfair. I am not saying I am better than others, but my Red Level gives me quite an advantage."

"Every game has a chance for the underdog, even if it is simple, perhaps especially so," the weapons master said cryptically. "Will you refuse a challenge?"

Chip thought about it, then sighed and shook his head. "I will not refuse a challenge. You have trained me too well."

He winked at the weapons master, who nodded.

"Good. Even a lesser challenger is good practice. We must attend a council meeting. Good day." Xander and Garth took their leave.

Ethrang, standing to the side, stared at Chip. "Wait, you must duel today, or you will be out of the tournament, right? I would challenge you, but since you look tired, I will wait until you are stronger," he said it seriously, patting him on the shoulder. Chip could not tell if he was joking or not.

Kristan and Thomas arrived all smiles. "Great show," they said, slapping Chase on the back simultaneously. "You are lucky it was Storm and not us." They tried to keep serious faces but failed. The twins looked at Chip. "We overheard that you must duel today to keep your spot."

Mina stepped in. "No, he challenged Gob yesterday to duel today, and the bully declined after Chip taught him a lesson."

"I can second that," Siz said, standing beside Mina. "Gob did refuse the challenge after he was knocked out and came to his senses, so to speak." He looked at her and smiled. Mina smiled in return, which made him happy. Chip looked at Eleanor and raised his eyebrows. She covered her mouth, trying not to laugh.

"That is true!" Ethrang shouted. He danced around excitedly. "That means you are still in the tournament!" Siz looked at him with disgust.

The twins stared at the blond boy's antics, and then Kristan asked, "You arrived a couple of days ago, if I am not mistaken?" Ethrang stopped dancing.

"Yeah, so?"

"Have you dueled yet?" the twin asked.

"I am duelling at lunch. It will be easy. I do not even have to use my special talents," he boasted.

"What talents?" asked Mina dreamily, looking up at him. Siz scowled.

"Oh, you will see. I only use my skills when I need to. Anyway, I am going now to prepare. Watch if you want," Ethrang said and scurried away.

"I will," Mina called after him. Siz had a look of jealousy.

Kristan stared at them quizzically then shook his head, "And I thought we were strange," he said, glancing at his brother. Thomas laughed, and they started walking off. "We have to go find someone to challenge. See you later." Kristan waved, not looking back.

As it turned out, challenges were ramping up throughout the day. They wandered to the Wizard's Duel area, and Mina explained Chip's challenge to the referees. They agreed it was legitimate and accepted the witness accounts. They made it clear that anyone caught lying would be disqualified. Gob happened to be in the area with Bart and verified that he had declined the offer.

"I heard what you did today," Gob said. "I do not need my butt kicked again. Besides, Bart is stronger than me and is fighting soon." He slapped Chip on the shoulder and walked off.

"That looked like it hurt," the queen whispered in his ear.

"Obviously," the boy answered. "He is like a small tree." They laughed. The referees stood up to make an announcement.

"Up next is Ethrang from the Green Level, who challenged Bart from the Brown Level. Take your spots."

Chip looked in surprise at the others. It seemed early in the tournament for a Lower Level to challenge a Higher Level. Then again, they were talking about Ethrang. Chip smiled at the wild boy, who gave him a thumbs up.

The two combatants faced each other in the white circle. Students passing by stopped to spectate after noticing the Guardian and the now famous Protector, Chase Longfellow.

"The rules are simple," shouted the referee, a plump woman in a blue robe. Her voice cut through the crowd like a knife. "No wizard's fire. No killing blows. Simply push or strike your opponent until they are out of the circle." Beside her sat three Yellow healers, sitting cross-legged on the grass.

"I hope Ethrang knows what he's doing," Chip murmured to Eleanor. Bart was cracking his knuckles in anticipation, eyes flaring a medium brown, looking at the skinny blond boy with disdain. The orphan stared at Chip for a moment, and then his eyes exploded bright green with a sheen of silver.

"Begin!" the referee cracked, standing with fists on her hips at the boundary line.

Bart threw his hands forward, sending a wall of air at Ethrang, but the boy had already dived to the right, making a swiping gesture with his left hand as he rolled. A loud pop sounded as Bart's right leg snapped at the knee, bending at a right angle. He bellowed and fell sideways, face contorting in pain, but managed to throw another stream of air before he hit the ground.

Ethrang dove left this time, but the air caught his foot, spinning him around. He took it in stride, landing cat-like, facing Bart with a grin. He swiped his other hand, bending the larger boy's left arm at the elbow and snapping it like a twig. Bart cried in pain and disbelief. Lying on his side, he tried to use his hands, but one was useless, and the other pinned.

"I will kick your ass when I'm healed, you skinny runt," Bart screamed hoarsely. He freed his remaining good hand and launched a fistful of air at Ethrang's face. This time, the blond boy enveloped himself in a thick green shield, blocking it easily. It seemed he had already determined that his green was stronger than Bart's brown, and he was right. The blond orphan walked up to him casually, eyes blazing, and waved his fists several times in the air.

Solid, compressed air battered Bart's face like real fists, slamming his head side to side. Blood gushed out of his mouth and nose. He tried to mount a defence but was too dazed. The green-robed boy stood over him, staring down. The brown fire left Bart's eyes, betraying his fear. Ethrang looked at him curiously, then extended one hand and levitated him into the air, walking him to the border of the circle. He placed the larger boy carefully on his one good leg.

"I have fought people much tougher than you," Ethrang said, letting go of his magic, eyes returning to a light blue. Bart managed to stand for an instant, giving the skinny boy enough time to reach back and unleash a full overhand right fist to the bigger boy's jaw, sending him flopping onto his back out of the circle, out cold.

The referee lifted her eyebrows.

"Winner!" she declared, raising her right hand to point at Ethrang. The young blond boy smiled and waved at the crowd. There was some tentative clapping, and then everyone joined in. Chip could tell many students were re-evaluating the potential damage a Green Level could inflict.

The other referee wrote the result in her duel book and closed it.

Healers ran to Bart and crouched beside him, sending yellow magic into his injuries.

Ethrang walked over and stretched as if he had just woken up. "Easy peasy," he said. "You ain't seen nothing yet."

Mina and the others congratulated him. Siz stood off to the side, pretending to look at the grass. The blond boy noticed and smirked.

A woman walked up to Eleanor. She wore blue robes with white embroidery on the sleeves. "I am Mary. I challenge you to a duel."

She was tall and lithe, with long black hair. Chip had to admit she was incredibly beautiful, almost exotic. Her eyes slanted like a cat's, and her olive skin was smooth. Chase stood transfixed, staring at the woman like he had never seen one before. Chip nudged him, and he snapped out of it.

The queen immediately assumed a confrontational stance, instinctually defensive. Chip wondered how women seemed so much more intuitive than men. Almost no words were spoken, yet she assessed the situation instantly. Looking at the woman standing before her, Queen Eleanor paused for a moment, making her wait, then answered crisply, "I accept."

Mary turned, approached the plump referee, and pointed at Eleanor. The other ref at the desk scribbled down their names, consulting a list. The woman walked back over with a tiger-like grace.

"We are next," she said shortly. Mary seemed to be in her mid-twenties, but looks could be deceiving.

Chase stepped forward in his usual awkward manner, oblivious to the unspoken messages passing between the two females, and asked how old she was. Mary glared at him and turned away. Chip rolled his eyes.

The referee stood up. "The next match is between Mary, the Blue Wing Leader, and Queen Eleanor of Vanalon. Take your positions, ladies."

She went over the rules. As she did, both women seized their Power, facing each other in the middle of the circle. Mary seemed slightly taken aback by the queen's intensity but hardened her features. She stood with feet wide apart, fingers splayed. Her eyes blazed a bright blue.

"Begin!"

Mary extended her hands, throwing her Power at the queen before the woman referee finished the word. Eleanor scrambled to form a thick shield, which she barely erected in time, absorbing the onslaught of compressed air. The queen raised her head and pushed back, blazing brown eyes glinting with red chips. Everyone gathered could see Mary's shock as she became overpowered.

Eleanor walked forward, both hands raised, and slammed Mary's arms straight down by her sides. She lifted the Blue Wing Leader off the ground and pushed the woman to the edge of the circle. The blue-robed female tried to envelop herself in a shield, but it did no good. Her face became frantic. Eleanor walked up to the struggling woman.

"You were rude to my Protector friend. He asked how old you are."

"I arrived here five hundred years ago," Mary answered venomously, "when Vanalon was a dirty village, bitch."

"You will address me as Queen Eleanor in the future." With that, she flung the Blue Wing Leader violently backwards out of the circle. Mary toppled end over end and finally landed in a scissors position, with one leg by her right ear.

The crack as her leg broke was audible to everyone gathered. The queen turned without a second thought and rejoined the group, ignoring the screams of pain. The crowd whispered, and scattered applause erupted. The healers ran to the shrieking woman, who could not untangle herself.

"Let's go," Eleanor said. "I have had enough of duels today."

Chip kept pace beside her. "What's wrong? Do you know her or something?"

"Yes," the queen responded shortly. "She was an advisor to High King Dominor when we visited the royal court a number of years ago. I was a little girl. I heard her calling Vanalon a backwards village and saying not to waste time with those mountain barbarians."

"Oh," Chip said, nodding. "I get it. Well, you showed her."

"It will not be the last we see of that conniver." She smiled, looking at him. "Just another enemy we have to keep watch for."

They went back to the dining hall in the Brown Wing. Chase accompanied them, and they walked up to Miss Highbrow, sitting at her seat, observing the students.

"Hi, Miss, this is Chase," said Chip, introducing his friend.

"What do you want?" she asked crisply. "I am trying to eat." The boy noticed she had a small piece of bread in front of her, which she had cut into tiny pieces with a knife and fork. He raised his eyebrows and continued.

"Right, well, I wanted to say that he is now my Protector and will be living with me." Chip was trying to be as polite as possible.

"Excuse me?" she looked at him as if he was a Yellow Level who did not belong. "Only Browns are permitted in the Brown Wing." She put her knife and fork down. "How on Earth can a student be assigned a Protector? You are not even a wizard yet!"

At that moment, a young green-robed boy appeared in front of the desk holding a letter. It was Ethrang. "Hi, guys, like my new job?" He beamed, handing Miss Highbrow the paper. "I am the new mail clerk. The cleric pulled some strings because I know you. I can enter any wing and drop off mail. I only have to work a few hours a day. If the letter is not marked urgent, I can deliver it anytime it is convenient for me. This one is marked urgent."

"You are so lucky," Mina gushed, smiling at him.

He looked at her coolly. "I learned a long time ago that you make your own luck. Wanna go out some time?"

Chip heard Siz gasp behind him, and he stifled a smile.

"Yes, absolutely. That would be great. Wonderful!" Mina exclaimed then looked around and blushed.

"Cool, I can get you later this afternoon, and we can challenge someone to a duel or something," Ethrang grinned.

"That sounds great!" she laughed.

"What? Can't you tell he's hiding something," Siz accused. "Stay away from him."

Ethrang turned, and a dark look flashed across his face. "I challenge you to a duel tomorrow."

Siz puffed out his chest then blanched. "I..." He looked like he was about to soil himself. "You are bullying me. I refuse." He looked about to cry and stalked away to the rooms.

"Well, it looks like I have the day off tomorrow. Wanna hang then, too?" Ethrang asked, trying not to laugh.

"Um...alright," Mina said, looking after Siz and seeming unsure of what happened.

"Ahem," Miss Highbrow was staring at them all in disbelief. "Do any of you know what protocol is?" She had the letter from Ethrang open in her hand. The Wing Leader looked at Chase with distaste. "It seems once again we are breaking the rules. I have...been ordered to allow your Protector to reside with you," she sniffed to Chip. "I will have a cot added to your room. I am certainly not going to give him his own room. I will add this to my list of things to deal with at the next council meeting." She returned to her piece of bread and began nibbling on a tiny square.

Ethrang looked at Miss Highbrow funny, snickered, and turned away.

"Alright, see you soon." He flashed Mina a smile and disappeared around the corner. The brown-haired girl held her expression and sighed explosively when he was gone. She started whispering to Eleanor, and then both of them giggled. Chip looked at Chase, and they both shrugged.

The lunch table was only half full that day, as many students were still at the Trials, observing the spectacles. Some came up to congratulate them, depending on which event they saw. Afterwards, Chase got himself set up in Chip's room. It felt like old times again.

"I have to make sure I pass my Trials," Chip said apprehensively.

"Huh, it will be easy for you," Chase assured.

"Not if they keep raising the bar to the point that no one can pass, not even me. I saw what they did to you too. In my First Trial, she made me lift a stone one thousand feet! That's insane. Then, to boot, I had to hold up the giant finger of the wizard statue while still trying to control it. Geez." Chip could not help but laugh. "Then again, I caused the finger to break off by resting the silly stone there in the first place. You had it much worse. I have to admit I would have failed."

"I was fine until Bulch stood up. He was a giant. He likes me now, though." They both laughed.

"Well, no more duels for me today. I am going to try and nap. You?" Chip asked.

"I'm going to wander. Maybe see what Mary is up to," Chase winked at him. "I'm not tired. Whatever you did to me made me stronger in every way. Thanks." He paused, "I wonder if I will live longer too."

"That is very likely, but none of us will live unless we find these Light Elves and hatch this dragon." He patted the pouch at his waist. "And see this Red-Eyed King, who will probably try and kill me. Then we just have to fight the Demon King and win the Last Battle."

"Piece of cake," Chase said. "Don't forget about the Dim. Are you good by yourself, Master Wizard?"

"Don't call me that. I am not your master, nor will I ever be. You are a human being. Guardian, wizard, or plain Chip will do, Mr. Invincible Protector."

"Yes, Master," Chase laughed, then slipped out of the room before Chip could throw something at him.

He fell into a disjointed sleep. His dreams were of magic and dragons, battles and wizards, and a Red-Eyed King beckoning him to an Ancient City.

10

When Chip awoke from his nap, it was nearing dinnertime. He met up with the others, and they decided to stay in for the evening. The companions enjoyed a nice dinner and played various games in the common room. Mina talked about her day with Ethrang, and the silly things he did to make her laugh.

Siz decided to join them but looked sour. Jordy came by to tell them he was running the Second Trials the following day, which involved setting a dining room table with the Power. It was designed for students to master the finesse of their abilities. They all agreed to give it a shot.

The next day, everyone completed the Second Trial, except for Siz, who seemed down and reluctant. He told everyone to give him some time to build up his confidence, and then he would partake. They left him alone after that.

The Second Trial did not involve a great Power output, so they decided to complete the Third Trial the same day. It involved healing someone else's wounds. The test had to be completed with a partner. Deep incisions were made in each person's skin. The wounds needed to be fully healed with the Power.

It was an equal test of pain and healing. Some students balked at such a task and even threw up at the sight of blood. The tester told them they needed to overcome their nausea and fear to pass the Trial or be barred from the Power. That spurred them to ignore their revulsion and complete the task.

The second phase of the Trial involved healing a pig's heart. These organs were by-products of the slaughter process, donated by the pig farmer who supplied the Guild. The dead hearts were punctured with a knife, and the students had to repair the blood vessels and entry points. In the end, they had to make the heart beat by pumping blood through it with the Power. Though it was difficult for some, everyone who partook passed the test. Chip and Eleanor had practiced with the real thing in battle over the past month and completed it easily.

Later in the day, the Guardian and queen received challenges to duel from a boy and a girl, respectively. Neither had any difficulty winning their matches. Ethrang got a pass because he had challenged Siz the night before, who refused. Both boys had not talked to each other since, which made conversations somewhat awkward at times.

As evening approached, they returned to the common room to discuss the day's events until the dinner bell rang. They were all digging into the evening meal when Miss Highbrow interrupted the service.

"Ahem. Excuse me, students. I have news." The Browns all turned, waiting silently. The Yellow and Green students serving the food stopped as protocol dictated. "I would like to introduce a new student." The Brown Wing Leader stepped aside to reveal a thin young man with dark hair and brown eyes. This is Petar. He just joined us from Calgar. He will see the Assessor tomorrow and don his brown robes. Please make him feel welcome. Have a seat." Petar shyly took a chair at the end of the table, avoiding eye contact. "The next piece of news is grave indeed and related. I am afraid the demon army has attacked Calgar."

Petar looked up with sad eyes and nodded. There was something strange about the young man, but Chip could not identify it.

"The initial reports suggest the demons number over ten thousand, controlled by three Inner Circle and a large number of Dark Elves. We have bolstered Calgar's defences with a score of Guild members and Protectors. I will keep you updated. For now, focus on your Trials and continue to practice. Jordy and the other senior students can assist you with your deficiencies. That is all." She returned to her desk and began cutting up a small piece of bread.

Chip and the others introduced themselves to Petar and asked him about Calgar. He seemed reticent to talk and gave vague answers, suggesting he wanted to be left alone. They gave him some space and finished their dinner.

Later, the group huddled in the common room, discussing the poor Calgarians and the demon threat. The students knew they had to harden themselves for the upcoming battle. The mood was somber. Chip felt tired, so he bade everyone goodnight and went to bed early.

The next day, the Silver Sword tournament began. Over one hundred Protectors entered. Each day, they would be halved. A poster displayed the duels. Carvor and Chase were purposefully put on opposite ends of the tournament board in anticipation of a meeting in the finals, though there was no guarantee. The rules were simple. The first to five points wins. An attempted death blow, if accidental, would cost a point. If intentional, the combatant was eliminated from the tournament. If a death resulted, they would be banished from the Guild. All victors would continue to fight until the seventh day when the math dictated that only two would remain. Both Chase and Carvor easily won their first-day match.

Chip decided with the others to take the Fourth Trial, which involved duelling a High Level designated wizard. The student did not have to win but needed to score well in strength, speed, adaptability, and control. The Fourth and Fifth Trials were both subjective. The tester decided whether the student passed or failed. If the student beat the Higher Level, they automatically passed. This did not happen often throughout the Guild's history, as the Higher Levels were chosen from the very best. However, it was possible.

Skylar was the designated wizard for the day. The old Seer

watched the group approach with disdain. A crowd had already gathered behind them. Chip was going to turn around and try it on a different day when Skylar was not around but decided not to show weakness. The boy tried to act civil.

"Good morning, Grand Wizard Skylar. How are you today?"

"Do not patronize me, boy. Have you come here to bully an old man with your Red Level?" he sneered. "It must be easy to walk around with a Level nobody has and breeze through life," he snorted. Chip's rage ignited, but he tried to quell it.

"Easy? I was an orphan and an outcast my whole life. I worked in the scullery for two years straight without a day off, then trained every day for six years living in the back of a stable." His voice increased in volume. "I have fought hordes of demons, Dark Elves, Inner Circle, and even a general. I've faced a black dragon, a creature called the Dim, and been hunted mercilessly. You call that easy, Seer?"

"Watch your tone with me, boy." Skylar looked down at him menacingly.

"Do not call me boy. You will address me as Guardian. Though I care not for rank, I will remind you I am only below High King Dominor and High Wizard Balor. My title was ratified by your superior. Let's get this duel over with."

Skylar's eyes blazed blue. "Yes, let's do that. Wizard fire is allowed in this Trial as we have protective shields."

"I do not need a shield," the boy said flatly.

"As you wish." Skylar draped himself in a full body shield, putting his head through the hole in the top. It looked to consist of metal covered in leather and almost went to his feet. He took a spot on one side of a large circle in front of a fenced-off area. His eyes blazed as he surrounded himself in a thick blue shield. A group of Yellow Healers stood to the side. "Stand on your side of the circle. You will be tested on speed, strength..."

"Do I pass if I knock you out of the circle?" asked Chip, cutting him off.

"Yes...boy. Begin!"

Chip's eyes blazed to life, and he sent a fist of red Power at the Seer, which struck his shield with stunning force. It flung the old man head over heels to slam into the back fence, knocking it completely over. He lay on the ground, unmoving. The crowd stood in stunned silence.

This was a Grand Wizard second only to Balor. Chip sighed then pointed at the crumpled old Seer, seizing him with his Power and pulling him back to float before him. Skylar's metal shield had melted at the impact point, burning the skin on his chest. Chip had made sure to mix air and fire to lessen the force, or else the man would be dead. He had struck him once with a fist, quickly pulling his magic back. Even so, the old man was barely alive. Chip flowed his magic into the Grand Wizard's injuries, healing him. He set him on his feet and walked away.

"You may have passed this one," Skylar jeered as soon as he regained consciousness, "but you will fail the Fifth Trial of Fear. I have seen it in my Telling! You are unable to control yourself, boy. Your rage will consume us all!" The old man's voice reached a crescendo, and he began cackling. Chip kept walking without turning back.

The crowd parted when they saw the dark look on his face, giving him a wide berth. His friends joined him instead of taking the Trial. They knew Skylar would likely fail them for even associating with the Guardian. It was better to wait for a different designated wizard.

They ended up watching a few more duels before receiving challenges from various students. The field had whittled considerably, forcing students to challenge more difficult opponents. They all won easily, even Mina. She was stronger than her diminutive form would suggest.

The Wizard's Duel was now on its third day and had reduced the combatants to sixty from five hundred. Few Greens and Yellows remained. Ethrang managed to beat a weaker Brown student to continue his streak.

At dinnertime, Miss Highbrow again gave them an update. "The gates of Calgar have been breached three times, but the city holds.

Over twenty Guild members from various Levels are there to hold the monsters back. Five have already died," she said softly. "One was a Brown named Ella. She was a good student...that is all for now."

She hurriedly sat behind her desk, looking down, moving her small pieces of bread around with a fork. Chip felt a pang of sympathy for her. The other students kept the noise down during dinner as a sign of respect. The mood was again somber. The new student, Petar, sat by himself at the end of the table. When he finished eating, they all went over to try again to make him feel welcome. He was wearing a new brown robe.

"I see you saw the Assessor today. I am sorry to hear about Calgar. I assume you have family there?" Chip asked.

Petar looked at him timidly. "Just my...father."

"Did he come with you to the Guild?" Siz asked.

The young man looked fearful. "No, why do you ask?"

Siz looked taken aback. "I was wondering if he got out before the attack." He looked at the others with a puzzled expression.

"Look, you are safe here," Eleanor said, sitting beside him.

"No!" he screamed. "Get away from me!" Petar pulled his brown robe tighter so it would not touch her as he shrank back in his chair. Miss Highbrow looked over with concern. The queen got up and distanced herself, which seemed to settle the man down.

"What is wrong with you? What have I done to offend you?" Eleanor asked, her anger rising.

Petar shook his head, his dark eyes looking at her in horror. "It is all over you...everywhere." Chip felt a tingle go up his spine.

The queen looked down. "What is all over me?" she demanded.

He cringed and trembled, then glanced at her eyes. "Death..."

Chip felt his blood run cold. "What do you mean by that?" he stood up, staring at the thin, sickly man.

Petar lowered his gaze, wringing his hands. "I can feel it...sense it...my whole life. Not for everybody, but most people." His teeth started chattering.

"What are you saying?" Chip asked, getting irritated. "Speak plain!" Miss Highbrow looked up again.

"I see when most people are about to die," Petar finally said, his face ashen. Chip felt his blood go cold. He noticed the dark circles under the man's eyes.

"Are you ever wrong?" he asked quietly.

Petar shook his head. "Never."

Chip sighed. "Can you tell when?"

The man nodded. "Death has completely surrounded her. Any day now."

"Can we do anything to stop it?" Chip finally asked. He had hoped that her near-death experience in the cornfield had avoided the prophecy. Eleanor was saying nothing. She had a resigned look on her face. Mina and Siz both put their hands on her shoulders, faces showing sympathy.

Petar shook his head. "It always comes true, even when I warn people. That is why I did not tell you earlier."

"You knew?" Siz asked incredulously, almost shouting. Miss Highbrow began walking over.

Petar looked down, not answering.

"Well, maybe this time we can stop it," Siz said earnestly, ignoring the Wing Leader. He looked at Chip, his face full of anguish. "I do not want to lose any of you. You are the only real friends I've ever had." The overweight boy looked like he was about to cry. Mina watched him for a moment, then came forward, nodding.

Chip sighed. "Stay close to her the next few days. When Chase is not training or duelling, I will have him guard the queen. I will sleep in her room." Miss Highbrow began to protest. Chip looked at her with a glare that would have stopped High Wizard Balor. "It is for her safety. I will put a cot in her room. I will not be swayed on this. It will be temporary until this...death omen or whatever it is passes."

Miss Highbrow pursed her lips, then looked at Petar. "There was another like you in the Guild once," she whispered. "She could see Death on people. She was never wrong."

"What happened to her?" asked Siz with a terrified look.

"She killed herself," Miss Highbrow sighed, "Her nightmares... were too much for her." There was an awkward silence. "Very well,

Guardian. Protect her if you can." She turned to Petar, looking at his dark eyes, a deep look of sympathy on her face. "Before bedtime, I can give you a tea that will help." He nodded and looked down.

"Is he a Teller?" Mina asked the Wing Leader.

"No. They are called Death Watchers. Most people do not even know they exist." She put her hand on his thin shoulder. "We are here for you."

"How long have you been a Death Watcher?" Eleanor asked.

Petar looked at her with sad eyes. "Over a century." They all looked at him in surprise. He looked to be about twenty summers old. This made sense if he found his Power at fifteen or sixteen summers. Then again, nobody likely knew how long Death Watchers lived.

"Why did you leave Calgar?" Chip asked.

His face looked haunted. "I lied to you about my father. He died long ago, as did my siblings. My mother at childbirth. They kept my secret during their lifetimes. I lived with them in a small house in Calgar, rarely venturing outside. I made sure to have no friends and never left without a hood, hiding the fact that I aged so slowly. Recently, I began to see the Death Shroud on everyone in Calgar, even the children. I could not take it anymore." He paused, remembering something. "Also, a little boy told me to leave. I see everyone as a vessel approaching death, even children, yet he looked crystal clear. It was like a sign. He said it was important to go to the Guild, and I believed him."

Chip shared a look with Eleanor. "Did this little boy have a sister, by chance?"

"Yes, how did you know? He called her...Beth. He was holding her hand. They were in the care of an older woman with greying hair. I did not get the little one's name."

"His name is Han. He is a Teller, or Seer if you will," Chip explained.

Petar's eyes widened, "There are no Seers that age."

"Normally, no. He is special, different. He sees things others do not. I hope your coming here will change the queen's fate, but so far, all it has achieved is to warn us. I pray that will be enough to alter it,"

Chip hoped. The young man looked doubtful. "Why have the people of Calgar not evacuated already? I do not understand."

Petar thought back. "Most did before I left. The diehards will not go, even if they have families. Some still do not believe the demons exist. I left about two weeks ago, before the attack. Most of the people remaining will stay."

Chip nodded in understanding. "I have heard that one before." He stood up. "Well, thank you for telling us the truth." He was about to walk away, then paused, looking at Petar. "How far in advance can you tell if someone is going to die?"

"Usually a few weeks at most. I only see it on certain people. It gets stronger as they get closer to death."

"How strong is hers?" Chip asked, pointing at the queen.

He looked over, then shuddered in fear. "It is imminent, but it fades in and out. Someone is going to kill her but has not decided when. I have seen this before when somebody is about to be...murdered."

Just then, Jordy walked up to them, catching the end of the conversation. "What's this about someone getting murdered?" he asked, laughing. He looked at their deadly serious faces, then dropped his smile. "What's going on?"

They filled him in, and he sat down in surprise.

"Wow. I have never heard of a Death Watcher. Weird."

"Aren't you supposed to be administering the Second Trial?" Mina asked.

"I...kind of shut it down to eat dinner." He looked around. "I get hungry too, you know. I will go back after."

Miss Highbrow reminded Petar of the tea and then looked at the others. "Keep your wits about you. Be careful who you duel with." She was going to say more then walked away and sat behind her desk.

Chip turned to Eleanor, "No more duels." She started to protest then saw his look and realized he was right.

"Fine," she said sulkily. "I was having fun, though."

"It will be interesting to see who is next to challenge you, Queen

Eleanor. Perhaps they have murderous interests at heart," Jordy said between mouthfuls of chicken soup.

"Let's stay in tonight," Chip said, deciding to take no chances. They all agreed, except Jordy, who had to go to work. Ethrang dropped by the front entrance to pick up Mina, and she told him the situation, saying she preferred to stay with Eleanor for the evening. He looked at her oddly then shrugged and left. They managed to get Petar to open up more and even play some board games. Several times throughout the evening, he actually laughed.

Later in the night, Miss Highbrow stood in the hall while Chip pulled his cot over to Eleanor's bedroom and moved his belongings. For now, Chase had his own room. The old woman gave the Guardian a reproving look, making sure he would not try any funny business. He could not help but grin as he waved good night.

Chip thought he saw her thin lips curl up slightly in a smile as she turned, but he could not be sure. The boy respected her wishes and stayed there talking to the queen for a good hour before kissing her good night. The kiss may have been longer than normal or more than one, but he was not counting.

They awoke and washed before breakfast. When all the students arrived in the dining hall, they heard a familiar throat clearing. "Ahem." Everyone stopped talking and turned to Miss Highbrow, who stood before her desk. Chase was mesmerized by the story of her eating little bits of bread and tried to figure out if she consumed it for breakfast too. He craned his neck to see what was on her desk, but she blocked his view. The Wing Leader noticed his antics, gave the tall boy a reproving look, then moved to block her desk further.

"Good morning, students. Grave news. Calgar has fallen." Everyone looked at each other in shock. "The last message we received from the besieged city was from King Henry, who stayed behind until the end. Demon reinforcements arrived in the night, and they surrounded the city, cutting off escape. The beasts attacked all at once. The king described several unique demons with terrifying attributes that turned the tide, but he did not elaborate. All the Guild members are dead."

She whispered a prayer to the Creator. "We do not know if the demon army will now march straight to Toron. If they do, we will meet them there and defend the capital. Our strategists suspect they will wait until the barrier falls, but nobody knows. We have scouts that will update us. That will be all."

She walked over to Chip and leaned down. "The High Wizard has requested you meet him in the Blue Hall." The boy nodded, looking immediately at Eleanor. "By yourself," Miss Highbrow added. "Do not worry. We will all watch her in the common room until you return." He was about to protest but figured she was in safe hands. He reluctantly agreed.

"Make sure she does not leave your sight," the boy said solemnly.

"That is my job, dear," Miss Highbrow assured him with a suffering expression. "Now, hurry along. High Wizard Balor does not like to wait."

He nodded and wolfed down one more strip of bacon before kissing Eleanor on the cheek and hurrying towards the door. He looked back once to see Mina placing her hand reassuringly on the queen's.

11

The Guardian exited the Brown Wing in front of the main gates. Ethrang was waiting there and looked surprised to see him.

"Hey, you are up early," the blond boy said, acting jolly.

Chip looked at him, a slight suspicion forming. "What are you doing here?"

"Oh." Ethrang looked startled by the question. "In Banfar, if you ask that people stab you." He laughed, but it died off. "Actually, I was just waiting for the Brown Wing to finish breakfast, and then I was going to ask Mina..." He seemed to grope for words, which Chip found odd. "...if she wanted to hang out or something." He finished, smiling weakly. He noticed Chip's suspicious look and then became defensive. "Why are you looking at me like that? It will only take a moment. Alright, fine. I like her. Happy?"

Chip remembered Siz saying there was something off about Ethrang. He arrived from Banfar on the same day they did. His mind raced. Could it be?

"I'll tell you what. How about you come with me to see the High Wizard? It should be interesting. It won't take long, and then we can see Mina together. I can help you get her to leave the queen so you can spend time together."

Ethrang thought about the request for a moment then shrugged. "It's always interesting to see what you are up to. Let's go."

Chip smiled, feeling relief. He was likely just worried over the whole Death Shroud thing, but it was better to be safe than sorry. He did not want more people around the queen than necessary, especially if he was not there. Chip led the green-robed boy into the Blue Hall. Ethrang looked around in wonder at the plush carpets and gold doors. He peered into the numerous alcoves, which held priceless works of art.

Chip looked at him. "I thought you delivered the mail. Have you not been in here before?"

Ethrang looked guilty for a moment. "Well… The truth is I only deliver for the Brown Wing. I said it to look important. When I got the job, they told me I would only be responsible for delivering to one wing, and I chose brown because I knew all of you were there." Chip frowned. "What? Your group is the most interesting, and you cannot deny it."

Chip stared at the blond boy. "I won't argue with that." He forced a smile, but he did not like that Ethrang lied to him. It made him wonder what else he had lied about. They ended up traversing the hall with no sign of Balor. Chip knocked on the gold doors at the end. Within moments, the cleric peered out.

"Ah, Mr. Guardian. The High Wizard was going to speak to you here but decided to change the location to the pavilion where he holds the Fifth Trials." Chip felt a bit exasperated. He did not want to be away this long.

"Fine. I will go now. Thank you."

"Go through this door here, and it will take you out." The cleric pointed to the left. Both boys nodded and exited the Blue Hall.

By this point, they were almost at the end of the Guild yard and only had to walk a short distance to the pavilion. It was a large white tent structure at the west end of the courtyard. The entrance was only a flap, so they pushed through and abruptly stopped.

"Cool," breathed Ethrang.

The pavilion was deceptively large. High Wizard Balor sat in a high chair at the far end of a small arena. Skylar and Xander sat in smaller chairs on either side. Maxim stood to the right, behind the High Wizard. Garth Stone was on the opposite side, behind Xander.

"Come forward, Guardian. We have been expecting you. Tell your friend to wait outside," Balor directed. Chip turned and told Ethrang to make sure he waited for him at the entrance to the pavilion. The boy nodded with a grin, then quickly backpedalled out. "Come closer." Chip walked until he was about twenty feet away. "Perfect. How are you doing?"

"Fine, High Wizard," he answered formally. Xander's face had an unreadable expression. Skylar's held a perpetual sneer.

"Miss Highbrow came to see me today. She relayed the information brought by the Death Watcher," Balor said, studying the boy. Chip blinked. "Those types of people are extremely rare. There is even a theory that wherever they are is where Death will seek. This man came from Calgar, and now everyone there is dead. I am not suggesting he brings Death here, but it is better to be aware. In any event, how is Queen Eleanor taking the news?"

"She is brave and, like me, hopes it is not true. If it is, she accepts her fate."

"Do you?" Balor leaned forward.

"No."

Skylar snickered. "See?"

"Silence!" Balor commanded, making the old man bow his head. He looked at Chip. "Do you believe in life after death?"

The boy looked at him, beginning to suspect where this was going. "Yes."

"Why?"

"I have seen it. I sensed the souls through the Divide as a young boy."

"Ha, are you so sure?"

Chip did not answer, waiting to see exactly where he was heading.

The High Wizard continued, "The darkness or entity we call Death is not what any of us think. We are mere paltry humans compared to that force. The representation it shows us is likely a construct of our minds. It might not even be real."

"What is your point?" Chip asked. Skylar gasped. Xander hid a small smile.

Balor ignored the breach of protocol. Proving his point would be more important than etiquette. "If it is not real, can you be so sure life exists after death?"

"It does."

"How do you know for sure?" the High Wizard pressed.

"Because I have seen Him."

"I told you that Death may not be real," he repeated icily. Chip's anger stirred.

"I am not talking about Death," he said louder.

"Then, who could you be talking about?" Balor laughed.

"The man with the silver hair." The High Wizard's laughter failed. Xander's eyes widened. Skylar looked skeptical, unsure of what was happening. Balor glanced at his brother shrewdly, noticing his reaction.

Xander's looked up at the boy. "What did the man with the silver hair say to you? It is important." Chip was unsure if he should answer. It had been such a special moment that he did not wish to share it. He regretted even bringing it up. "It is alright. I have seen him too." Chip stared at the wizard in astonishment. Balor gave a start. "He told me one day, I would know when to share my story. That day is today. Not even my brother knows." He leaned forward. "It was two nights before we erected the barrier." The High Wizard looked over in surprise. Chip knew Balor was thinking of his last conversation with his father, Arkan, which happened one night later. "I had gone to sleep and suddenly awoke in a white room. A park and a bench appeared. I stared at a beautiful tree in the park, and when I turned back, an old man was sitting on the bench in a white gown..."

"With long silver hair." Chip smiled at the memory, remembering the feeling of peace.

"He asked me to sit," Xander said, lost in reverie. "I did, and he told me a great sacrifice was necessary to reset the Balance. My father needed to make it, not me or my brother. He said I should share that knowledge with my father, Arkan. It would remind him of an important Telling. He would know what it meant when the time came. The man with the silver hair said nothing is certain, but a semblance of balance can be restored if all goes right. One day, it will fail again. He said the two sons of Arkan must lead the world one last time to stop a complete failure of the Balance. If the Laws are breached, a reset will be attempted in the form of a child, a babe with red eyes. I must find him or all is lost before it has begun. If the Dark defeats the Light, the Balance will break. The Nothing will then rule all. Fear its touch. There will be clues in the Tellings, but not the answer. The answers are in the Balance."

The wizard stopped talking, letting them absorb the words.

Balor looked at him accusingly. "You gave that message to our father. He told me he would make a sacrifice the next day...and gave me the Galad Prophecy. I never fully understood what it meant."

Xander nodded soberly. "I did. I had to."

"How do you know that?" yelled Balor. "We could have saved him!"

"You know that is not true. Let us listen to the boy's words before we try and understand." Xander looked at him coldly. "You also never told me you spoke with Father the next day." The comment finally settled the High Wizard. "The one clear thing is Skylar's warning that I not see the Galad Prophecy because I might prevent Arkan's sacrifice is unfounded. In fact, the opposite is true. The man with the silver hair felt I needed to know to remind my father of the Telling."

Skylar gave Xander a hateful look. "I can only interpret a Telling to the best of my abilities. Besides, other knowledge in the prophecy could have affected your actions. Finding out through this so-called man with the silver hair may have been precisely what you needed. Your belief in this...dream person seems profound and affected you differently than if you read it from an old parchment."

Xander stared at him. "You have an answer for everything, don't you?" Skylar narrowed his eyes.

Balor just shook his head and turned back to the Guardian. "Very well. Speak."

"All of you should remember we fight for the same cause," Chip said. "You both loved your father. Be happy you had one."

Skylar made a choking sound. "How dare you...."

Balor just looked at him. His glower even caused Maxim to raise an eyebrow. He turned back. "Speak."

"I met the man with the silver hair when I seized my spirit essence in the throne room of Vanalon," Chip recounted. "I was going to use it to save the princess." Skylar arched his eyebrows and glanced at Balor. "The old man said true courage is not being afraid to be vulnerable." Chip thought hard. "Death is a force that embodies the absence of Life. The man with the silver hair is the opposite. Death and Life cannot exist in the same spot."

"Anything else?" Balor asked.

"He said the bench in the park is always there. I used it to tether my spirit essence to find my way back. I surrounded Morgo's body with it and destroyed him. Morgo was made of Death and could not exist in the same spot. The old man gave me the clue, or I think he did. Time froze when we spoke. He called it an eternal moment. I could have stayed there forever. It was so peaceful. So when you ask me how I know there is something more after death, that is how."

The High Wizard nodded. "Good. I wanted to see how strong your belief is. You experienced Death and Life already, so you should believe." He paused. "I ask these questions because the Tellings, the Galad Prophecy, and now even the Death Watcher have all indicated the queen will die." He gave the boy a piercing look, and then his voice took on an edge. "My father gave his spirit essence so that humanity would survive. I do not want his death to be in vain." Chip finally saw where he was going and began shaking his head. "Hear me out, Guardian. I need to know that for the sake of us all, you will let her go!"

"No!" Chip yelled, rage igniting. His eyes blazed red. "Never!"

Balor stood up. "Fine!" he roared, eyes exploding with blue magic. Skylar and Xander looked at him with fear. Chip could tell that nobody had ever seen him that mad. "Then you better find a way to save her!"

Chip stood there for a moment longer, breathing hard, staring unflinchingly at the High Wizard of Amrika, eyes blazing. He turned on his heels and walked away.

"By the way," Balor yelled after him. "You have failed the Fifth Trial!"

Chip kept walking, not caring. He broke through the pavilion flaps into the yard. Ethrang ran up to him and stopped, seeing his blazing eyes.

"Oh dear," he said.

Chip was not in the mood. He did not release his Power. "What special abilities do you have, Ethrang? Why were you skulking around the gates, trying to get into the Brown Wing? Why did you follow us from Banfar? Were you in a cult? Do you work for the Demon King?" The skinny boy looked caught off guard. An expression of guilt and fear washed over him. Chip had never seen him scared before. Now, he did look like a lonely orphan. His suspicions were confirmed.

"I...was in the cult for a time... We all were... I never killed anyone, I swear. And I left the cult before you arrived, then I heard your speeches and believed there was something more..." he said haltingly, not looking at him. Chip could tell he had done bad things and was not revealing everything. His rage did not diminish. They walked towards the middle of the yard.

"Tell me the truth. Do you work for them?" Chip asked between clenched teeth.

"Work for whom?" Ethrang demanded.

"You know who—the Dark Elves. You said you have special abilities. What are they?" he yelled. A crowd was growing around them.

Now it was Ethrang's turn to get mad. "Why don't we find out?" he shouted, seizing his Power. His eyes turned bright green with a hint of silver.

The crowd started chanting, "Duel! Duel! Duel!"

Chip, for once, could not agree more. "I challenge you to a duel!" he yelled.

"I accept!" Ethrang screamed back.

They both strode up with blazing eyes to the referees, who looked at them in shock. The plump lady was about to yell at them to get in line, then saw Chip's demeanour. "I have challenged him to a duel," he said through gritted teeth. "Now."

"Well, first off, you are more than two Levels apart..." she began.

"I do not care!" he shouted. She was about to scold him, Red Level or not when the second referee raised her hand.

"Wait," she squeaked. She was a tiny girl with glasses. "We are now down to thirty combatants, so the Two-Level rule is gone. They can challenge whoever they wish."

The plump lady stared at them both. "Fine. It looks like you are... ready. Take your spots. Let's get this over with. Try not to kill him," she added under her breath.

Chip and Ethrang squared off against each other at either end of the white circle. The skinny blond boy actually had a grin on his face. "You asked for this, Guardian." The crowd went berserk.

Chip felt a twinge of doubt for the first time then discarded it in his rage. He would blast this Demon King worshipper into oblivion.

"Begin!" the referee yelled.

It was mid-morning in the Brown Wing. The group lounged on the couches in the common room, waiting for Chip to return.

"Alright, that's it," the queen said. "I have waited long enough for him. I cannot hold it anymore. I have to pee." Miss Highbrow raised her eyebrows, which made Chase laugh, given her name.

"He said not to move," the Brown Wing Leader reminded her.

"I am not going to pee on the couch!" Eleanor protested. Chase laughed again.

"I can go with you," Mina offered quickly.

"Oh, if you really cannot hold it, I will go too." Miss Highbrow stood up.

"Looks like we are all going," Chase said, unwinding his long body like a cat, then stretching as he rose off the couch. Petar agreed to come too.

"Fine," Eleanor said, "but girls only in the washroom." Mina smiled.

They got up and escorted her down the hall. Siz sat alone on the couch for a moment, looking after everyone as they started walking away, and then rolled his eyes. "Wait for me!" he called. Chase told him to hurry up before running to keep up with the queen.

The group walked through the double doors to the bedrooms. The two private washrooms were at the end of the hall. Chase ran up, inspected the one on the right, then nodded for Eleanor and Mina to proceed. The girls giggled as they entered. Mina turned back to look at everyone with a smile as she slowly closed the door and locked it.

There were two windows on either side of the hallway for air. Chase looked out the one on the left, which looked over the interior courtyard. He could make out two tiny figures duelling in a little circle in the middle. Oddly, he thought he could see a green and red robe in the circle, but that didn't make sense.

From here, the Protector arena looked like a little box. He was told to guard the queen, so all avenues had to be checked. Miss Highbrow stood in the middle of the hall with Petar and Siz behind her. He decided to look out the right window as well. Chase could see the front lawn and the Ancient Forest from this view.

He knew they were in the brown robes of the woman wizard statue at a height higher than the wall. Well over two hundred feet up in the air. It was quite a fall. He heard a strange sound and turned to look back down the hall.

"Begin!" the referee yelled.

Chip, brimming with Power and rage, unleashed a torrent of solidified air at the skinny boy in green robes. He was so mad he almost released wizard fire but remembered the rules. The air was so condensed it could easily be seen with the naked eye as it hurtled towards Ethrang. Nobody in the Guild could stop such Power.

Then the blond boy disappeared. The crowd gasped as one. For a moment, Chip thought he had obliterated him but realized Ethrang had vanished. He dropped his hands, looking at the referee. Suddenly, a huge mountain wolf appeared in front of him at full speed, slamming its shoulder into his chest with stunning force. He tried erecting a shield as his body flew backwards, but it was too late. He landed on his back hard, losing air. For a crazy moment, he thought Silvermane had come back to life. Chip looked up to see the huge wolf gone and in its place a charging buffalo that kicked him in the butt hard, sending him tumbling end over end. He finally formed a shield as he stood up, ignoring the pain, hands ready for whatever enemy was before him. Instead of a charging buffalo or mountain wolf, a young green-robed boy stood laughing at him.

"I win," Ethrang said, pointing. "You are out of the circle."

The crowd was silent, digesting what happened, and then everyone started shouting.

"He beat the Guardian!"

"He turned into a wolf!"

"That skinny kid just beat the Red Level!"

"He's a shapeshifter!" the plump referee exclaimed in shock. "Ethrang wins!"

The crowd started clapping and patting the boy on the back. Ethrang walked over to the Guardian, who stood in disbelief. "I told you I had special abilities."

"How?" Chip managed, releasing his Power.

"I dunno. I was born with it. If you notice, there's a silver sheen to my magic. I thought someone was going to figure it out. That's why I wanted to challenge hard people like you first. The element of surprise is very important," he said smugly.

Chip's mind whirled and raced. Ethrang could be anybody, including a Dark Elf. "How do I know you are who you say you are?"

The blond boy's face suddenly turned cold. "You don't."

"Are you really from Banfar?" Chip asked, watching his reaction.

"Yes."

"Why did you follow me here?"

"To kill you." the green-robed boy said and clenched his teeth. His eyes blazed silver-green. The crowd gasped.

Chip looked at him in disbelief and seized his Power in response. "I guess you can try." He formed a thick red shield, waiting for the attack. "So you are a Demon King worshipper too?" he accused the shapeshifter in a menacing voice, his rage growing.

The blond boy stood there with hands in fists at his sides. He changed his shape into a multitude of different forms before finally turning into the street urchin Spider. "He was my friend. We were like brothers," the young thief cried.

Chip looked at the small boy, and a wave of shock, sadness, and guilt washed over him. The street urchin then transformed back into Ethrang, who looked at the Guardian with grief and rage. "You killed him!" he shouted.

Chip's mind reeled in confusion.

Ethrang continued, "Spider and I were both orphans. He was younger than me, so I took him under my wing. We grew up on the streets of Banfar. The cult gave us food and shelter. We worked for them, bringing in converts. I found my Power two years ago and began to distance myself. Spider did not want to.

"The Dark Elves showed up a couple of months ago and began hurting people who would not convert. The horrible old elf Bashan arrived and used that chamber in the cavern below the altar. Spider brought him victims to torture and enjoyed watching. He became more evil by the day. I separated myself from the cult but did not give up on my friend. Then you arrived and destroyed the Dark Elves. I was happy about that until I found out you killed Spider too.

"When you left Banfar, I followed you to get revenge for my friend's death, but I was confused because you did many good things. I decided to watch for a while before making up my mind."

Tears ran down the blond boy's face as he recounted the story. The orphan stood before him, the bravado of the street kid gone. In its place stood a lonely boy stripped of all his barriers and pretenses.

Ethrang's eyes blazed with sorrow, yet underneath it was a simmering rage.

Chip looked at him with regret, feeling a heavy weight of sadness. He dissolved his shield and released his Power. The red fire went out of his eyes. The young boy's face widened in shock, realizing the Guardian was now defenceless.

"I share your sorrow, Ethrang," Chip said, his eyes tearing up. "Spider tried to stab the queen while she was lying on the altar. A man named Quirk tried to kill her at the same time. The only thing I could do at that moment was to throw a red shield around her. Spider jumped on Eleanor with his knife raised and died instantly from the Power. I am truly sorry, my friend."

He looked at the blond boy with haunted eyes.

Ethrang stood before the Guardian, eyes blazing, knowing he could kill him right there. The orphan from Banfar stared at him for a long moment, tears streaming down his young face, before nodding and unclenching his hands. The silver-green magic in his eyes flickered and went out. "Spider became evil by the end," he sighed. "I am not even sure I could have saved him, but it was hard for me to let go. He was like a little brother. Just so you know, I decided a while ago that I wouldn't kill you, Guardian. I know you have a good heart and would help anyone, even me. Besides, you have become my friend."

The two boys looked at each other with sad eyes. Ethrang reached out impulsively and hugged the Guardian, letting go of vengeance. Chip returned the embrace, feeling a sense of relief and forgiveness. The two orphans formed a strong bond in that moment, as each forgave the other. The students around them nodded in approval, knowing that two powerful individuals had formed a meaningful connection.

A nagging thought entered the forefront of Chip's mind, and he pushed the green-robed boy to arm's length, looking into his eyes. He was missing something. Ethrang looked at him oddly. It was something to do with the blond boy's...Power. Then it hit him like a club.

Somebody else had silver in their magic.

"Siz has a silver sheen too!" Chip shouted.

Ethrang looked at him in alarm, stepping back. "Nobody told me that." He slapped his forehead. "That is why he has never used magic around me. I would have recognized him instantly as a shapeshifter. Mina told me Siz was always saying something was wrong with me, that he couldn't put his finger on it, but he knew exactly what the silver meant. Siz was lying."

"Siz is a shapeshifter," Chip said slowly. The words sounded weird to him. "He followed us from the cornfields. Siz said he is from Thundar but could be…anybody."

"Right. I can be anybody too, but I promise this is the real me. You can tell if I show you my memories." Ethrang looked nervous for a moment then sighed. "Fine, there are things I'm not proud of, but check if you want."

"That's alright," Chip said reassuringly. "Your offering is proof enough. Our memories should be our own. Right now, Siz or whoever he is could be alone with my queen."

"Let's go. I have a surprise for you. I noticed a beautiful red unicorn when I followed you in the Ancient Forest. I could not resist landing on him as a fly. Now I can be him. I'm the fastest horse in town!" Ethrang laughed and shapeshifted into Redmane.

Chip let out a whoop and leapt onto the red unicorn's back. The crowd looked on in wonder as the mighty beast sprang across the yard at breakneck speed towards the Brown Wing.

12

Siz smoothly pulled a dagger from his waistband as Chase stared out the window overlooking the Ancient Forest. The overweight boy turned back into Murk as he calmly drove the blade to the hilt in the back of Petar's neck, killing him instantly. Before the body hit the floor, he turned into one of the deadliest demon scorpions ever created. The Dark Elf used his claw to swipe the side of Miss Highbrow's head with vicious force, sending her careening into the wall, fracturing her skull. Chase turned in time for the stinging tail to whip down on his chest with bone-breaking speed, sending the Protector flying backwards through the window. A surge of joy rolled through Murk. This was the only part of the plan he was not sure about. With his advanced abilities, the Protector was a terrifying foe, but the Dark Elf had timed it perfectly.

Eleanor and Mina, hearing the commotion, wrenched open the door to find Siz crying, pointing at the body of Petar. "He fell!" As the queen tried to move forward to help, Siz turned into the demon wasp from the cornfields and drove all five talons deep into her chest. Mina looked at him in horror, seizing her Power. He pointed at the small girl with his left claw, shooting a torrent of brown fire into her body. She tried to build a shield, but he overpowered her, slamming her back against the wall. She lost consciousness and collapsed, burnt and smoking. Eleanor tried to bring her magic to bear, but Murk yanked his talons out of her chest, causing the queen to scream in pain and fear, blood spraying everywhere.

She sank to the ground, struggling to breathe, unable to seize her Power. He sprang over to the window and peered outside. On the ground far below was the tiny, unmoving body of the Protector, his legs bent at odd angles. Murk sighed with relief, then spun back. Eleanor again was trying to summon her magic, which he knew was formidable. His wasp armour would only protect him so much. He reached across with a claw and backhanded the side of her face hard, knocking her unconscious. The faint fire went out of her eyes.

Thankfully, no other student had entered the closed double doors at the end of the hall. In the mid-to-late mornings, pupils were usually out in the yard or training downstairs. They had been the only ones in the common room when the group had gone to the washrooms. Soon, though, the others would be coming back for lunch. His last goal was to knock the Guardian unconscious when he arrived and fly away with him. After that, he would give the boy sleeping herbs until he awoke before his Master. He tried to smile, but the demon wasp was not built for such a facial expression, so he switched back to his natural Dark Elf form.

Murk congratulated himself. He had waited patiently to make his move, gathering information. The Dark Elf looked at Petar's dead body. The Death Watcher had foiled his plans, forcing him to act quicker than he anticipated. As an assassin, he had immense patience but also knew when to take advantage of windows of opportunity. Petar's warning drastically reduced his chances of isolating the queen from the Guardian. It was fortuitous that the High Wizard had summoned the boy this morning. Murk could not let such an opportunity pass.

Taking the form of Siz was frankly exhausting. An overweight human boy with all kinds of fears and anxieties was a challenge. He had found him in Thundar after Murk received rudimentary healing from the inept town healer. The man paid the ultimate price for his lack of skill. He assumed a dead soldier's form and walked to the general store after spending the night in the dead healer's house. He was consuming disgusting human food next to a fisherman's cabin at the back of the store when he noticed an overweight boy use Brown Level magic to clean one of the boats. The father was nearby but did not notice.

Murk had called the boy over and gleaned important information regarding the town and current affairs. The boy was a whiner, physically weaker than his peers, but his magic was quite strong. The beginnings of a plan formed right then in the Dark Elf's mind. It was a contingency plan if the boy wizard and his companions reached the Guild before he could achieve his goal. He allowed his creative juices to flow, weaving an intricate web. Assassination required careful planning.

He asked the boy personal questions about his fears and thoughts, building the character in his mind. His name was Siz or Ciz. He had no idea how to spell it. The boy was firm that he would not go to the Guild to be trained for fear of being bullied, so Murk decided to take his place. He shook the boy's hand, waved to the father, and then walked out of town. He tried the new human form out, turning into...Siz. No one would suspect him. It was perfect.

Murk smiled in satisfaction. Things were now going according to plan. He walked over to remove the dagger from the base of the Death Watcher's head. He could hear Eleanor gurgling as she drowned in her blood. Miss Highbrow was in a crumpled heap, likely dead. Mina was unconscious, still smoking from her burns. He walked back over to the queen and knelt beside her.

She regained consciousness enough to look up at the shapeshifter groggily. He revealed his yellow, pointed teeth then dug a finger into one of her wounds, making her squirm, and licked the blood off. He tilted his head back in ecstasy. She cried weakly in pain. Murk chided himself for giving in to his desire for human blood. He should end her quickly and move to the next part of his plan.

Then again, harvesting her organs would only take a few

moments. It was nearing lunchtime anyway. He set himself to the task, bringing the knife to bear. Murk salivated in anticipation.

Suddenly, the doors to the hallway burst open to reveal the red-eyed Guardian and Ethrang. The Dark Elf hissed in shock and lifted the dagger directly over the queen's chest.

"Do not move, or I will stab her heart. Your magic will not reach me in time, I promise you," Murk said with vicious intent.

Chip's rage was palpable. "Do not hurt her," he warned.

"It's too late for that," the Dark Elf cackled. He watched as the boy looked around, surveying the situation. "Oh, if you are looking for your friend Chase, he's dead. I am afraid he took a bit of a fall through the window."

Chip reeled with anguish. Ethrang noticed Mina behind the Dark Elf and cried out, starting to move forward.

"Stay where you are, shapeshifter, or she dies too." The green-robed boy froze. "I am surprised you have the ability. There has not been another for millennia. It seems the Balance is always at work, but this time, it is too late. I do not think you realize the advantage you have, boy." He paused. "I have to ask, how did you figure out I was Siz?"

"The silver sheen," Ethrang said, "only the two of us have it. The Guardian did not know until I shapeshifted in our duel just now. Who are you?"

"How rude of me. I am Murk of the Inner Circle. I know all of you," he laughed wickedly. "I enjoyed taking out your guards one by one across the plains and then ridding myself of that pesky wolf." Chip bristled with rage. Murk smiled at his reaction. "You humans are so odd." He turned to the blond boy. "Out of curiosity, did you win your duel?" Ethrang nodded. The Dark Elf laughed sharply. "Shapeshifters, especially when their abilities are unknown, are gods. You should have kept it to yourself, boy."

"I never liked Siz. Now I know why," Ethrang spat.

"Oh, Siz is still alive," Murk chuckled. "He is the son of a fisherman in Thundar. He is a Brown Level, and since he refused to be trained at the Guild, I figured I would take his spot. It worked almost perfectly until you two came along. But...you are still too late. Looks like the prophecies are right after all."

With that, Murk drove the dagger straight into the queen's heart.

"Nooooo!" screamed Chip. His magic flew out uncontrollably, bursting doors and knocking Ethrang sideways into the wall. Murk turned into the demon wasp and dove for the open window. Chip would have been too slow, but his rage had already extended his magic to fill the entire hall. He directed his fury at the disappearing wasp, seizing its tail with a red hand and pulling back. Murk screamed and sent all his Power towards the boy, trying to break free. This time, he miscalculated.

Chip held on to the Dark Elf and enveloped himself in his Power. The full force of Murk's magic struck his shield with no effect. He felt something snap in his mind, and his magic increased to fill the new void. He was growing stronger. Ethrang watched as the Guardian strode in full fury towards the struggling wasp and shrank back against the wall.

Murk's body transformed into different shapes as he wriggled in the air, desperately trying to break free. The demon wasp turned into the scorpion, then a spider, then a host of other monstrosities, and even tried disappearing into a fly. It was to no avail. Chip had him fully surrounded with his red Power, so the monster had nowhere to go. The Dark Elf kept changing, even turning into Eleanor for a moment, as the vice tightened. Finally, Murk stopped moving and shifted into his true form, facing the Guardian with a sigh of resignation.

"I have completed my duties, human scum. Her death fulfills the prophecy. You will help my Master destroy the world with your rage. Then you will die..." His pale, scarred face broke into a wicked smile, showing his pointed yellow teeth.

Chip moved forward one more step. "No. Your Master will die, just like you." The Guardian cupped his hands together, filling Murk with tendrils of red magic until he was full, then extended his fingers in all directions, ripping the Dark Elf apart with his Power. Murk screamed as his limbs flew off in every direction, burning into ash as they incinerated in the surrounding bubble of Power. The sound stopped as his face melted mid-change, turning into the Guardian himself, a final grisly farewell. He had made his last transformation. The Dark Elf was completely gone the next instant, vaporized by the intense Power. Ethrang ran to Mina's side, sending his magic into her body, desperately trying to heal her.

Chip knelt next to the queen, looking at her ravaged body. Her eyes were open but lifeless. The dagger protruded from her still chest. Eleanor's face was still beautiful, even in death, frozen for all time. The boy could not control his emotions. The look of her horrendous wounds was too much to bear, so he laid his trembling fingers on her body and repaired the injuries, as he did to Silvermane. His Power withdrew the dagger, which fell softly on the lush carpet beside her. He mended the gaping holes in her chest and then carefully reconnected the tissues of her heart. He forced all other thoughts out, as they were too painful to bear. Chip finished and looked at her in repose, beautiful and proud. Her sightless eyes stared at nothing.

The words of the prophecies and Tellings rang through his mind, predicting her death. He had tried everything to stop it, but it was not enough. Now his best friend was dead too. Chip turned his blazing red eyes to the heavens and let out a long moan of despair. The mournful sound echoed down the hall, telling the ultimate tale of sorrow and grief. Ethrang healed Mina, and both looked at him with tears in their eyes. The great Guardian was a young orphan again, a lost little boy, more alone than ever.

Chip gazed down at his dead queen, his one love, then stared at his hands. He could see the red envelope of Power surrounding them. All the magic he had was still not enough to save her. What good was it? He decided then and there that he did not want it anymore. The fools thought he would snap with rage and destroy the world. He had no intention of doing so. Instead, he would destroy himself.

Chip seized all the Power he had, filling himself to bursting, then directed it into building his Wall. He would make it impregnable, barring himself from magic forever. He emptied most of his Power into it, strengthening it almost to the point where he could not access it ever again, leaving one last hole to fill. The red fire died out of his eyes as he looked at his last little bit of magic.

Out of detached curiosity, he noticed that the Wall was strongest at its base, as all walls should be. Yet, the last bit, which looked like a small red brick in his hand, was the weakest. The boy knew that once he filled the last hole, it would forever stop him from getting through. He suspected someone stronger might find his weak brick and break it if they knew where to look. But no human was stronger than him, so he was safe. His magic would be locked away forever.

The Guardian turned the final small red brick over in his fingers, already beginning to experience the huge relief he would finally feel being free of the... responsibility. He paused, not liking the word. What was the saying? "The higher the privilege, the higher the duty." She had said it to him many times.

He looked at her dead face, imagining her saying it. He tried to shrug it off, rolling the small bit of Power in his fingers. What would he do after, anyway? He turned his head, looking at the open window and the more than two-hundred-foot drop, knowing his best friend was at the bottom. Nobody could survive a fall like that, not even Chase. Eleanor said she would wait for him. He knew his best friend would too. They would both be there. All he had to do was put in the last piece of the Wall so there was no turning back, then run and jump to freedom.

Tears streamed down his face. Ethrang was saying something to him, but he could not hear. He did not want to. He was about to fill in the last piece of the Permanent Wall, but something was bothering him. Something at the core of his being. He forced himself to remember. He looked through his memories and saw himself facing Death as a young boy. It was then that he promised he would never give up again. More tears streamed down. He had promised.

He had given his word.

Chip Oathbinder knew that in the end, at the core of his being, even with everything he loved gone, he had his word. He was his word. He was named after it, after all. How could he, of all people, break it?

If they managed to somehow win this war, the boy knew he would live longer than any human wizard. Chip did not want to live thousands of years without her. He groaned in anguish.

Yet... he had no choice. He gave his word. Her words again reverberated in his mind. "The higher the privilege, the higher the duty." The boy shook with rage. He hated that saying, yet he knew it to be true. The unfairness of it all fed his anger. He had tried his hardest, given everything he had, done all that was asked of him, and still lost it all. "No," he said to himself.

"No!" he screamed aloud in utter frustration.

"Fine! I will be your Guardian," Chip shouted to the heavens. In desperation, he pulled some bricks off the Wall in his mind and infused her heart with magic, making it beat up and down, pumping blood through her veins. Colour returned to her skin, but she would not wake up. He knew she would not. The queen's eyes were open and dead, seeing nothing.

He screamed again in rage, then remembered Balor's admonishment, "If you won't let her go then you better find a way to save her!"

Ethrang and Mina were trying to tell him to let her go, but he ignored them. Eleanor's body was healed, but her spirit essence was gone. The thought struck him like a hammer. He would find her spirit essence! He delved into her head with his Power, searching where her mind would be. There was nothing there. A deadly, empty coldness seemed to have replaced her. She was gone, completely. He felt his rage grow.

"Quiet!" he roared at Ethrang and Mina as they tried to explain it was over. Other students had begun entering the hall, but he did not care. He vaguely saw someone trying to revive Miss Highbrow. He was missing something. Something someone said. No, something someone wrote... the Galad Prophecy! "His rage can destroy all, Or his love can restore hope."

Love.

He delved deep into her cold head, remembering his love for her.

He saw dark tunnels leading to emptiness. Wait. There. One tunnel had the faintest residues of her spirit essence. It had passed that way. His love recognized her. He followed with his mind, pulling more bricks down to sustain him. The outside world disappeared entirely.

He went down the dark tunnel, seeing her residue increase slightly as he went along. It got colder and darker at the same time. He started to shiver, so he wrapped himself in more Power, which helped. His love for her guided him, revealing the faint essence of her passing. He went deeper, becoming aware that this was not a place for the living. His body seemed impossibly far away. Her passing was getting stronger. He knew she had been here recently. He followed deeper, his love giving him strength. The darkness became stronger too, thicker, almost suffocating. He knew he was getting close.

Finally, he reached a wall and recognized it. It was the Divide, the same wall he had seen when he was very ill as a little boy. He went close to it and peered through. There she was! On the other side. A small, bright light. Her face materialized as she looked at him through the Divide. He felt hope flare to life despite the numbing cold. Yet something was wrong. She was shaking her head. She was telling him to go. He could read it in her face.

"No." He spoke, but it carried no sound. Then he realized something else was there, an immense dark mass on the other side of the wall. With shock, he realized it was holding her there, baiting him. She looked sideways at it in fear.

It was Death, and it would not let him cheat it again. He knew it deep in his bones.

Yet he knew something else too. He was not like normal people. As Balor said, he would find a way. He reached out to put his hand through the Divide. The mass on the other side drew up, ready to pounce. Eleanor's spirit essence was screaming at him to leave. His mind raced. It was getting colder. He looked at the Divide again. It separated Death from Life. A realization dawned on him.

Death could not kill Life. She would not be able to exist on the other side if it could. The man with the silver hair had told him that Death could not exist where Life was. They could not be in the same spot. Death could only trap those behind the Divide, never letting them return, or at the least be the go-between from this life to the next. In Death's greed to get him, it held her spirit essence just on the other side. If it had let her move on, he knew she would have been lost to the world of life forever, but now he had a chance. Chip only had to reach through and pull her back, yet he had to do something first.

The boy formed his Power into a faint trail so he could find his way back to the Divide and returned swiftly into his mind, going through the hole in his Wall and diving into the core of his being. The white ball of his spirit essence appeared before him. He immersed himself in the brightness, and everything seemed to stop. The park bench was still there. He pulled the white light tight around him and tethered it to the leg of the bench.

"You cannot do this." The man with the silver hair stood under the perfect tree, which had appeared along with the rich, green grass.

"Why?" Chip turned to him.

"It is against the Laws," he said.

"So change the Laws."

"They are not mine to change."

"So who made them?" Chip asked in frustration.

The man with the silver hair sighed, stepping forward to stand before the boy. He looked at him with eyes like pools of infinity. Chip was overcome with love and peace. The other place was cold and empty, devoid of life. This place was warm and full, the essence of life. "There is a force that binds everything together. It is not alive as you see it, nor can I explain further. Your mind is not built to understand it. We call it the Balance. It has Laws. Death and Life are expressions of this Balance. It must be so, or else nothing would exist. If the Laws are broken or bent, the Balance is upset. If they are skewed too far, the Balance will break and all is lost. Everything that is, and was, and will be, all of it, is gone." He placed his hand on the boy's shoulder. Chip gasped as he sensed a jolt of unfathomable Power, seemingly infinite. "What you felt is the same on the other side. If you do this, Death will take you."

"To where?" he asked breathlessly.

The man with the silver hair looked at him for a long time, even though such a construct as time did not exist. Finally, he said. "It is belief that gets you there."

Chip thought he understood and knew the man would say no more on the subject. "The Demon King broke the Laws," he realized.

The old man froze. "Yes."

"So did Death," the boy said with conviction. "He cheated."

"He?" The man with the silver hair let out a musical peal of laughter. The sound made the boy grin despite the gravity of the situation. "You do not like to give up, do you?"

"I will not give up. I gave my word. I told you I will sacrifice everything for her," he said solemnly.

The old man's laughter faded. "Yes. You did say that."

"Perhaps this will right the Balance," Chip said.

"The Balance does not gamble."

"Do we not have free will?" Chip asked.

He studied him again. "That you must decide for yourself."

"Then I choose my free will. I am going after her." Chip pulled his spirit essence around him.

The man with the silver hair shook his head. "You have great Power, but you cannot withstand Death." He paused and sighed. "She might be able to, at least for a while." He pointed to the pouch at the boy's side then disappeared. Only the bench remained.

Chip made sure the tether was secure then pulled in a deep breath and dove down the faint red trail back into the darkness.

13

The Guardian of Humanity wrapped himself in his bricks of Power, pulling the formidable Wall he had strengthened in his mind around him like armour. He streaked through the dark tunnels, reabsorbing his red thread, desperately keeping the cold at bay. The Divide appeared before him again. He saw Eleanor's beautiful spirit essence struggling in the grasp of the force of Death and aimed for it like an arrow without slowing.

When he pierced the Divide, what he thought was cold before was nothing compared to the deep freeze of Death. He gasped in shock then swam towards her through the blackness. She met him halfway, and they joined together as one. Joy went through him for a moment as they reunited.

Then Death struck.

The force enveloped him like a black cloud so powerful it was beyond comprehension. He swam back towards the Divide with all his might, holding tight to her. His tether was already getting thinner, ready to snap. He reinforced it with his bricks of Power. Chip realized with icy cold fear that Death would not destroy him because it could not. Instead, its purpose was to cut him off from the world of the living. It wanted to keep him from ever living again.

At least he was with her.

Yet now, in the grasp of Death, Chip Oathbinder finally understood the true joys of being alive. His eyes were wide open to the preciousness of life, the vibrancy, the freedom, and the reality. He did not know what afterlife, if any, existed on the other side of Death, but he did know all the joys of living on Earth. A stark realization hit him. He loved her so much, but when one person is solely defined by someone else, if all their joy is wrapped up in another, then they are not truly living. There were so many other people and experiences to enjoy. He realized that now, in this coldest of places, hoping it was not too late to be alive again. The boy had been willing to sacrifice everything in the world for her, even destroying the Balance, all for his happiness.

For his selfishness.

He now knew life was far too rich and varied to tie it to one thing. Growing up as an orphan with no parents who loved him, he had put his happiness in the hands of others. He should have put it in himself. Only then could he really experience a loving, rich relationship with Eleanor. Together, they loved each other greatly, but the love of self was as important, if not more.

Despite his love for the queen, he should have been the foundation of his life, not her. If she died with a proper base of self-love, he should have been able to carry on. He owed the world a great duty. He would not shirk from it any longer. The Guardian would not forsake humanity ever again.

A conviction entered him that he did not have before. It was a sense of self-love and belief that gave him the confidence to keep fighting. The weapons master's wisdom came through, even in this darkest of places. *I am enough.* The orphan repeated it in his mind. He did not need others to make him happy.

He was enough.

The realization gave him strength. He may have foolishly given everything to get her back, but he was now going to make it worthwhile. She would help him save the world.

The boy pushed his Power out against the blackness with all his strength, following his tether back. Death fell on him hard, ripping his defences apart like paper, smashing his red bricks of Power. He saw the edge of the Divide in front of him. He was so close. She strained with him, together pushing against a sea of black. His hand touched the Divide as Death stripped him of his last bricks. A cold began to freeze him in place such as he had never known.

"I am here."

A female voice entered his mind as energy entered his hand and infused his whole body. It was the dragon.

She had awoken. He felt her Power cover them both in a white shield different from his. Instead of bricks, it was like white armour, like scales. Death seemed to slide off it, struggling to tear it apart. She was made of something different. Chip remembered the Balance had created her to fight the Dim, the Nothing. Death was not Nothing, but it was a force of emptiness, similar enough to give it pause. Wrapped in the new armour, they both kicked forward, pushing against the Divide. Death became agitated and frantic. It refused to let them leave. A monstrous weight tore at them, ripping apart their defences. The dragon wailed against the onslaught, scales disintegrating. With horror, Chip realized that even combined, they were not strong enough. Death was going to win.

Suddenly, something struck them from behind, pushing them forward hard enough to tear open the Divide. They turned around to see a white entity behind them, nudging them through. Eleanor and Chip jolted in surprise. It was the spirit essence of Queen Charlotte. Her smiling face was beautiful and peaceful, radiating light. Eleanor cried as their essences touched. An eternal moment passed between them that only a mother and daughter could share, and then Charlotte's spirit gave them one final push.

A wail echoed from Death's realm as they landed on the other side, hearing the Divide snap back into place. They watched Charlotte's spirit essence recede into the blackness, still smiling. They spun to follow Chip's white tether back through the cold darkness, feeling life slowly return.

Behind them, a horrible groaning sounded, and they looked back to see the Divide bulge and rip open. A scream of fury erupted from the darkness as a black figure crawled out from the hole. It was the embodiment of Death itself, and it was coming for them. Chip somehow knew this was very wrong and that their lives, even their souls, were in danger.

They frantically followed the tether back up through the dark tunnels. The black figure followed them, gaining speed, shrieking in rage. Just when it seemed the thing would catch up to them, they entered Chip's mind, and he pulled her spirit essence into his until they reached the park bench, surrounded by white light. A warm feeling of safety struck the boy, and he turned to see Eleanor beside him, looking more radiant and beautiful than ever. They existed in an oasis of white light.

"You saved me. You risked everything. It was too much, Chip. I would have waited for you." She gazed at him with her stunning blue eyes.

"You did risk too much," a rich female voice said, and they turned to see a majestic white dragon sitting on the green grass beside the perfect tree.

Next to her stood the man with the silver hair. "Too much indeed. Do you see now why love for another cannot be at the expense of everyone else, including yourself?

Chip nodded. "I see that now. I am sorry it took Death for me to truly see Life."

"It could be the most expensive lesson ever taught," the man with the silver hair mused. "Or maybe it was the only way." He smiled.

Suddenly, his smile vanished, and for the first time, his glowing face showed an expression of anger. "How dare you?"

The power in his voice was like nothing Chip had ever heard. At first, he thought the old man was talking to him but realized he was looking at something behind them. They turned around to see the black thing crawl grotesquely into the light. They stepped back as it grew in front of them, a cold draft preceding it. The thing materialized into a tall, black-cloaked figure.

The being pulled its hood back, revealing a man's smooth face with midnight hair. The eyes were black pools of infinities, similar to a demon's but far deeper. "I might ask you the same question." His voice was dead and cold. He looked at the man with the silver hair. "Interesting archetype you've chosen."

"I could say the same. It makes the most sense from their perspective. You have gone too far this time, Death," the old man said, his voice strong.

"You allowed, even assisted, in that which cannot happen. She was inside the Divide. You broke the Laws," the black being said coldly. "Is it necessary to speak in these forms?"

"Yes. It is, considering you are in his spirit essence. How is this possible?" the old man asked.

"There is enough space between their essences," Death said.

"I could cut your head off. You are in my realm now," the man with the silver hair stated ominously.

A high cackle that only Death could make came out of the being. "You know what that would do. Neither of us is that foolish."

"What do you want?" the old man asked.

Death pointed at the queen. "Her. She is mine."

Chip faced Death. "No."

"You said that to me once before." It looked at him curiously. The boy stared into the dead eyes of infinity and saw something he could not describe. "You dare gaze upon me, human. Only those who die can see me. You will release her."

"No." Chip stood his ground, knowing the force he was up against was beyond comprehension.

The man with the silver hair stepped in front of the boy. His face and demeanour exuded unimaginable Power. "You cannot have her. What is done is done. You have bent the Laws too many times. The Balance hangs by a thread. I offer this to square it up."

Death looked at the queen, then the old man, and smiled.

"Deal. You have miscalculated this time."

"I do not gamble."

The black figure chuckled then turned towards Chip. He felt

small and vulnerable. "I am inclined to tell the boy about the Great Forget."

"You could, but that is not your place. The cooling of the cosmos has changed you." The old man peered closer at the being. "It has... bent you. These matters are not your concern."

Death grinned then shrugged. "Your time is coming, Guardian. Earth will fall, then the next, and so on. It should have happened five millennia ago, but for this... event. I can bide. Time has no meaning to me." He looked at the Queen of Vanalon, who shivered. "Let us see if his...love...was worth it." He laughed again, a sound like dry bones rubbing on a tombstone, and started sliding down into the white floor. "The dragon was clever. I did not expect it." He disappeared.

The man with the silver hair turned, face crinkled with amusement. "Death will never know the power of love. Keep your faith in it." The old man looked at the queen. "You have a very important role, it seems. The Balance does not play dice." He turned to the dragon. "May I name you Starlight?"

"You may." The stunning white dragon bowed low. The old man smiled.

"So this did not break the Balance after all?" Chip asked hopefully.

"We will see when the queen returns to her body. It certainly will create a... ripple. You cannot fully understand, but this particular universe is held together by a number of constants. The forces involved are greater than you are capable of imagining, but they are balanced. If one of these constants varies but a little, everything will collapse or unravel. You will cease to exist. The Great Forget caused a ripple like no other. The Balance seeks to realign the constants.

"My opposite, what you call Death, is not the same as in the Beginning. It is growing, or bending, an awareness. The Demon King is an expression of that awareness. In their bending of the Laws, this king has attained Powers that no Earthly being should hold. Death seems to have taken an...interest, which should not be in its nature. This so-called Demon King is not significant to us in relative Power, yet he manifests this interest, making him more powerful than anything in the cosmos. He gives Death a taste for life, which goes against the natural order. If he wins, Death may morph into the world of life, and the constants will change, creating chaos and the end of all things. He is unable to see these consequences. He now seems…sentient beyond his purpose. So, in essence, Chip Oathbinder, you are not only fighting for your world, you fight for existence itself." That left them in stunned silence.

"I do not know if I am strong enough," Chip finally said, looking down. He suddenly felt the weight of everything on his shoulders. At that moment, even surrounded by the purest white light imaginable, he felt like a lonely orphan.

The man with the silver hair smiled and reached out to gently touch his shoulder. Chip felt an incredible loving strength infuse him.

"You are not strong enough, dear boy. It is true. Yet you are not alone. You have great friends, powerful Protectors, able magic wielders, and now you have her." He looked at the queen. "The Galad Prophecy came true. I knew it would. After all, I am the one who gave it to Galador." Chip looked up in shock. "Yes. There is a tiny amount of wiggle room between the constants. That is where prophecy comes in. The Balance works through me and in me too. I see now why she had to die. It was hidden from me before. Her death was not so you could learn about your rage. It was so you could learn about your love. Death showed you the final absence of life, the cold dead blackness, the emptiness, the nothing."

The boy looked up, thinking of the Dim. The dragon raised her head.

The reactions did not go unnoticed by the old man. "That is a different Nothing. No forces can exist there." He paused then looked at Chip with eyes of infinity. "You, of all the humans who ever lived, received the most valuable lesson of all. This experience changed you. It moved your spirit. You now understand what true love is. You were willing to sacrifice everything for her, yet now you see the preciousness of life itself. You see the folly of putting all your love in another. You now have a newfound love of life and of yourself. In the end, if you survive to fight the Last Battle Chip Oathbinder, you might be alone. Remember, you are not just fighting for her. You are fighting for all of us."

The boy nodded, tears in his eyes. He remembered the feeling of losing everything. He felt great shame for even thinking of barring himself from the Power and ending his own life. When he truly knew what Death was, he understood with stunning clarity the importance of Life. Now, more than anything, he did not want to lose it. He wanted to fight for it, not just for him but for everybody. He would always remember, every single day, to be grateful for it.

The man with the silver hair stood before the boy, looking at him with the mesmerizing eyes of infinity. "Nobody is ever alone, even an orphan. If you lose someone, then grieve but move on. Keep your gratitude, and you will find new love and joy. Seek help in your journey. Others will join you."

He looked at the dragon. "She will fight with you. The nothing of Death is not the Nothing of the Dim. That creature is a by-product of what you call the Great Forget. In essence, it was created by the Balance to counter the event. It is a true Nothing, fearful of Death only because that nothing still contains something, a force. It does not like that. It wants complete Nothing. It is the absence of everything, including all forces. There is nothing like it in the cosmos, and it is growing stronger. If it is not stopped, it will unravel the world and achieve a worse result than the Demon King's victory. They have worked together towards a common goal, but in the end, the Nothing seeks to consume everything.

"In the past, the Dim feared the touch of Death, a nothing it did not understand. The dead General Morgo used that fear to control it, but as it grows, even Death will have no power over it. It will grow larger and become unstoppable." He turned to the dragon. "You must stop the Dim. Your Power is different from all others. It helped the boy escape the nothing of Death, but that is not the Nothing of the Dim, which you are designed to counter. You know of what I speak." He sighed and looked around. "We all have our roles, even me. The odds are against us. Perhaps Death is right, and the Demon King will win. What Death does not realize, if it comes to pass, is that we will all lose."

The man with the silver hair turned and walked over to the park bench. "You will not need this anymore." He gestured, and the bench disappeared. Chip blinked. He looked at the boy once more with eyes like pools of infinity. "I will not speak to you again until the end, if at all. Remember, the Tellings fit into the tiny cracks of the constants. I have some small leeway to guide you, but prophecy can be misinterpreted to the point where sometimes it causes the opposite reaction." He laughed, the musical sound soothing their hearts. "The Balance seems to have a sense of humour." The man with the silver hair began to walk away.

"Who is Han?" Chip blurted before the old man left.

The question seemed to surprise him. He turned and said nothing as he studied the boy, then began to fade away. "He is the one who Tells true and clear, yet can only read the Paths the Dim does not close. He is closer to you than you think. He is...an expression within an expression. Heed him, but in the end, choose your own Path. After all, you are the Guardian."

With that, the man with the silver hair disappeared.

The others looked at each other. "Thank you, Starlight," Chip said to the white dragon.

She bowed her head. "I sensed your rage and your love. You could not bear the loss without the knowledge. We all have our paths. The journey cost me dearly, and I must rest again." Chip started to apologize. "Do not feel sorry, Guardian. It was necessary. I knew I would be needed, so I took the Deep Sleep in the first place. I will wake again in the presence of the Light Elves, but not before. If you do not find them, then all is lost. I cannot change this." She began to disappear. "I wish to fly in the winds of the sky." Starlight faded away.

The Guardian turned to his queen, gazing at her beauty. It was only the two of them. She turned her face to his and stepped close, blue eyes sparkling with a radiance he had never seen. Her soft lips parted, looking into his green eyes. He felt a sense of peace and joy like no other, surrounded by a sea of pristine white light. At the same time, their lips came together, and he kissed her for an eternal moment, all thoughts and responsibilities gone, replaced by pure love. Time did not exist, and the two became one, their spirit essences intertwining in the deepest sense of intimacy two humans ever shared. The moment felt infinite.

When it ended, neither knew. At some point, they disengaged, realizing that they were two.

"I love you, Guardian," she breathed.

"I love you too, Queen of Vanalon."

"You came back for me," she said, holding him tight.

"I did."

She cupped his cheeks in her hands, drawing him close. "Thank you, but do not ever do that again." She tried to stay serious but could not help it. He picked her up and swung her around, basking in the white light. "How much time do we have here?" she asked.

He laughed. "Here, time is frozen. We have all the time in the world. It is an eternal moment." Suddenly, he remembered the old man's words from the first time he was there. "Do not tarry too long, or you will not want to leave."

"We must go," he said with growing urgency. "It is too beautiful and perfect here. We cannot linger."

"I want to stay," she said, confused.

"So do I, but we cannot. Grab my hand." Yet even as she did, he wanted to stop and kiss her again. He wanted to stay. The world could wait. Chip started pulling her towards him, realizing he wanted to take her somewhere but could not remember. He decided it was unimportant, and then an image of Chase entered his mind, and a sadness shattered his indifference. He clutched onto the memory of his dead friend, which reminded him that he needed to leave, and pulled her with him, diving down into the white floor.

Chip felt her spirit essence separate and enter her body. He jolted back into his, and reality crashed down. All his senses flared to life, and for a moment, he felt overwhelmed, then his sight settled and coalesced into her face. She was still sprawled on the carpet in the hallway of the Brown Wing.

Ethrang and Mina crouched close, looking at him with concern. He could hear other students coming down the hall behind him. Several crowded around Miss Highbrow. He held the queen's hand and looked at her still face. She was not breathing. He tried sending his Power into her but had none to give.

"We need to start her breathing," he cried. "Ethrang, link with me."

"Guardian, she is dead. I'm sorry," the blond boy said to him with wet eyes.

"Listen, please trust me. Link with me. I am out of Power," he said earnestly. Ethrang shared a look with him that only two newfound friends could and extended his hand, his silver-green eyes flared to life. He asked no more questions.

Chip seized the young boy's Power, surprised at its strength, and directed it into Eleanor's body, forcing her heart to beat and pulling air into her lungs. "Breathe," he said soothingly. Come back to us." Nothing happened.

Then, there was a small flutter and another. Her eyes blinked and then opened. She took the breath of life. A bewildered look crossed her face until she saw him and began to smile. The queen opened and closed her fingers, breathing on her own. Ethrang fell on his rump in shock, eyes wide, while Mina shrieked joyfully. The other students gathered around, talking excitedly.

"The queen is alive!"

"She's awake!"

"The Guardian saved the queen!"

Cheers erupted up and down the hall. To their left, Miss Highbrow stood on wobbly legs after being healed, rubbing her head. "What on Earth happened?" Her glasses were askew on the bridge of her nose. Everyone laughed.

Chip realized he was still linked to Ethrang and turned to the green-robed boy. "That is quite a Power you have here. I see now what the silver represents. I will not look at your memories, but I sense we orphans have similar experiences. Thank you." He released the link.

The skinny boy grinned. "Anytime, Guardian. Orphans have to stick together." He laughed and looked at Mina, who hugged him.

"Ethrang, how did you turn into the wolf Silvermane in our duel?" Chip asked, his curiosity burning.

The boy laughed. "Easy, when I followed you from Banfar I noticed a large mountain wolf keeping pace. I can only shapeshift if I touch the person or creature I want to be. I was terrified of the wolf but wanted to take his shape, so I turned into a flea and jumped on him." The other students gathered around started smirking, thinking he was making a joke. "I ended up hitching a ride that day, but I enjoyed the form on other occasions. Truthfully, I prefer to be a giant eagle." He emulated a flying motion, then noticed the broken window on the right side of the hall, and his laughter died.

"Chase fell from there. I'm sorry, Guardian," he said somberly.

The other students gasped, offering condolences. Chip felt a great sadness descend on him, and tears filled his eyes as the full weight of his best friend's death struck home. The hallway door slammed again as more students entered, talking aloud.

"It would have been nice to get a little help," a voice complained from the end of the hall.

Chip's eyes widened, and he spun around. There, in front of the double doors, staggered Chase, limping towards them.

"You're alive!" Chip screamed, unable to control himself. He jumped up and ran into his best friend, hugging him fiercely.

"Ow. Geez. My legs are mending. When I came to, I had to straighten them with my own hands, then wait for them to heal. Do you have any idea how much that hurt?"

Chip laughed. "I am sorry. We thought you were dead, and I was kind of busy."

Chase looked at him suspiciously, "Busy doing what?"

"Oh, nothing major, just losing a duel to Ethrang, who happens to be a shapeshifter, then destroying another shapeshifter Dark Elf named Murk, who used to be Siz, then going through the Divide into the realm of Death to bring our queen back to the world of life, and finally having a deep conversation with Life, Death, and a white dragon in my mind, otherwise not too much." Chase blinked, making Chip laugh harder. "I will tell you all about it. Here, let me heal you."

The boy touched his best friend's shoulder and seized his magic. A tiny spit of red energy flew out of his finger. Chip looked embarrassingly at his hand. "Well, that's awkward. I'm afraid I'm a little low right now, my friend. Fighting Death took a bit out of me." He looked around. "Uh, can someone else heal him?" Ethrang and Mina laughed and pushed him aside, putting their hands on Chase's shoulders. They sent healing magic into the tall Protector.

"Ah, that's better," Chase said, stretching his legs when they finished. "So," he cracked his fingers, "is there anyone left to fight?"

Then, the tall boy noticed Petar lying off to the side. The young man's haunted face finally looked at peace. "Is he..."

"Yes," Chip said. "The shapeshifter killed him. He can finally rest."

Chase nodded. "I saw a demon scorpion come at me, striking me with its tail. I flew out the window and fell for a long time. I managed to put my legs under me to protect my head, and then everything went black. I guess I have a pretty hard head."

"That is definitely true," Chip said, smiling.

Jordy suddenly burst through the doors, looking around in confusion. "What did I miss?" Everyone looked at each other and laughed.

At that moment, a vibration went through the Wizard's Guild. An unseen ripple passed over them like a wave. Reality itself seemed to waver, and then it was gone. Everyone looked at each other with relief, knowing they were lucky to be alive but unsure why.

14

Thirty leagues to the southwest, Han stopped his horse in its tracks. The wave swept over him. He sensed what it was but could not describe it with his young mind. The little boy waited, unsure if it would pass, and then exhaled when it did. Han and his companions had been riding to Toron. His sister sat behind him, tiny hands clasped around his small waist. The capital was still three days away. They had been travelling from Calgar for over two weeks. He looked at the bright sun of midday, then watched the wind ruffle his horse's mane.

Auntie Clare stopped with him. "What was that?" she asked, looking at Han.

"A change," the boy said. "A necessary one." He turned and looked at her solemnly. The two soldiers, Neb and Jon, stood patiently to the side. They had learned very early that the little boy was different. "The Paths have changed." He stopped again and looked inward then gasped. "They need to know!" He felt Beth scrunch her little face against his back to avoid a gust of wind.

"Who needs to know?" Auntie Clare asked.

"The Guild and the Guardian," he said as if it was obvious.

"Who on Earth is the Guardian?" Auntie Clare asked.

The little boy barely heard her. "I know where they are, or at least where to find them," he said excitedly.

"Where who is?" she asked in exasperation.

"There is a great danger too. The Balance has responded." His small face went serious.

"The what?"

"We must go to the Wizard's Guild now. They need to know." He started turning his horse.

"Han, we are only three days away from the capital. Surely, it can wait." She tried to reason with him, but he shook his head.

"We must go now."

She looked at the little boy and sighed. The boy laughed as his sister made a face at her. Auntie Clare finally smiled and nodded. "You two are very special. Very well. After you, lad."

Han gave her a grin, then kicked his horse, turning to the northeast. The boy made sure his sister held on tight as he urged his mount into a trot. His mind continued analyzing the new Paths. Han knew he would dream when he slept that night. It would be the most important dream he ever had.

WORD SPREAD that day in the Wizard's Guild of the shapeshifter Murk trying to kill the Queen of Vanalon. The fact that a Dark Elf had infiltrated the Guild scared the students and teachers alike. Balor called an immediate meeting of the council. Chip and the others who were present described the morning's events in detail in the council room. The wave or "wavering of reality" event, as some called it, caused concern. Skylar used it to justify that the boy had made the wrong choice in saving the queen. Balor recognized that, based on the words of the man with the silver hair, it was likely meant to be. In fact, the High Wizard had been an unwitting participant by screaming at Chip in the pavilion earlier that morning, shouting that the boy had better find a way to save her. That led to another talk of whether any of them had free will at all.

In the end, they decided to finish the tournaments and reconvene three days later to determine how to find the missing Light Elves. The council had finished analyzing the histories, and no reference was found to their mysterious disappearance.

The next morning, a funeral service was held for Petar. The young man's face looked peaceful in repose. Chip could only imagine what a cursed existence he must have lived. He whispered a prayer to the Creator that the Death Watcher's spirit essence find solace.

That afternoon, Chase and Carvor met each other in the finals of the Silver Sword tournament. Chase won five points to one, becoming the youngest Protector to win the Silver Sword in the history of the Guild. Garth lost by one point to Maxim, allowing the master trainer to vindicate his loss from many years prior. When the boys asked the weapons master why he did not seem up to his standard form, he winked at them, saying it was important for the current master trainer to teach his students confidently.

They did notice Maxim's mood had changed, and he seemed a little nicer. Besides, Garth noted, they were now tied at one win apiece, and there was nothing more exciting than watching a third match in the future.

In the Wizard's Duel Tournament, Ethrang beat Thomas in the semi-finals, turning into a fanged black bear and sending the blonde twin careening into the crowd. Thomas was a formidable Blue and tried to wrap the skinny green-robed boy in a bubble of Power, but Ethrang's intense green magic sliced through. From there, he charged at the twin. The impact sounded throughout the yard, but Thomas survived, only sporting six broken ribs. The orphan raised his hands to the sky and leapt into the air as a ferocious brown tiger. The crowd erupted with applause and began shouting, "Ethrang, Ethrang, Ethrang!"

In the finals, the boy shapeshifter met Kristan, the stronger twin. When the match began, Kristan immediately surrounded the wriggling green-robed boy in a thick blue magic bubble. Ethrang disappeared into a fly but was surrounded. Though very powerful, his green magic was not strong enough to slice through Kristan's shield. In a panic, he changed into all manner of beasts and birds that wowed the crowd, but in the end the twin levitated the skinny boy and cast him out of the circle. When Kristan released the bubble, Ethrang shapeshifted into a giant eagle and flew high in the air, letting out a mighty shriek of frustration. He then returned to the middle of the circle, folding his great wings and bowed his eagle head in deference to the new champion.

Kristan received the Wizard's Duel Crown, and both twins were granted a seat on the council for their performances. Chip received an invite along with the queen, Ethrang, and Chase.

The day of the meeting dawned bright and sunny, but soon, dark clouds began to roll in, and the sky darkened. The wind picked up, growing in intensity.

A storm was coming.

After lunch, everyone convened for the important council meeting. Chip still felt awe every time he entered the opulent room. They all sat in their appropriate sections at the hexagonal table. Chip had the lone red seat. Chase stood behind him to his right. He had earned admittance, as he was now a Certified Protector, not to mention the Silver Sword Champion. Eleanor sat in the Brown Section with Miss Highbrow and Jordy. Kristan and Thomas sat between Xander and Skylar in the Blue section, along with Mary, the Blue Wing Leader, who gave the queen an icy look. Ethrang, for his unique abilities and strong performance in the Wizard's Duel Tournament, represented the Green. Beside him sat his Wing Leader, a middle-aged man named Pete, whose hands rested on his large, round belly.

Rumour had it Pete enjoyed an excessive daily amount of mead, which he produced from honey collected in the Ancient Forest. The Wing Leader Magda, the older woman who ran the First Trial, represented the Yellows. She was flanked on both sides by two top healers, Connie and Dorothy.

"Good day, council members," High Wizard Balor began. "I have convened this meeting to discuss the Guild's next steps. Some of you are new to this council and, going against protocol, I have invited you based on your ranking, abilities, and performance in the tournaments. I am not so old and foolish that I will only hear advice from those who have been with me the longest. I know the value of new ideas, thoughts, and opinions. Times have changed, and the Guild must change with them." He glanced at Skylar, who bore his traditional sour expression. "Calgar fell days ago, and thankfully the demon army has not yet proceeded to the capital. Instead, they have retreated to Cave Mountain, where they will likely await their Master, the Demon King. Our scouts monitor them from a distance. All humans are dead from Vanalon to Calgar. The demons hold the west. We must find the Orb of Power to have a chance against this growing threat…"

The doors to the council room burst open, and the cleric appeared, hair dishevelled.

"How dare you?" Skylar yelled at him.

For once, the cleric completely ignored him. "High Wizard, something is happening in the sky far to the west." He took in a breath. "And a party of travelers are coming across the bridge from the Ancient Forest."

Balor read the fear on the cleric's face, then leapt to his feet. "To the wall!" They all filed out, rushing into the great Blue Hall and climbing the stairs two at a time. The council reached the top of the Guild wall to see many students pointing and shouting. They ran to the edge, two hundred feet above the ground, and gazed at the western horizon.

Dark clouds covered the sky, blocking the midday sun, and a strong wind blew. The sounds of thunder cracked overhead. To the west, bright white lights were shooting in the sky, incredibly distant. Chip sensed a deep, powerful magic being released, the like of which he had never felt. To sense it from this distance was almost unfathomable. Balor and Xander stood side by side on the wall, faces stern.

"It is the barrier," Xander's voice shook. "The Wall holding back our greatest enemy is breaking apart."

"Our father has held him back for three thousand years. His strength has run out," Balor said sadly, his face faintly lit up by the lights far to the west. As if on cue, a small light shot towards them from that incredible distance, growing brighter. The students pointed in wonder. It arced across the Earth from west to east, travelling at blinding speed. It seemed to dim as it headed straight for the Guild as if it was running out of power. When it reached them, it had shrunk to a small ball of light that stopped before Balor and Xander. The two brothers stared, not in fear but in wonder and disbelief. Two pieces of the ball broke off and went into the bodies of the two wizards, who stood side by side, transfixed.

As the light entered Balor's chest, he sighed, as did Xander. The remaining small ball of light floating in the air suddenly transformed into a see-through image. A figure with long white hair stood before them, wearing a white robe, smiling.

"Father!" Balor gasped, weeping openly.

"It is you!" Xander said, eyes streaming with tears.

The two old men were like boys again, looking up with admiration and love at the man who had raised them.

Arkan looked at his sons for a long moment with utmost love and raised his hand in farewell. His image fragmented into tiny bits of light and disappeared. The other students looked on in silence, many with tears, knowing they had witnessed something profound. Xander and Balor looked at each other, not as two powerful wizards, but as brothers. They clasped one another at the same time, a comforting embrace of loss and love, as their father's life energy returned to the cosmos.

A murmur erupted throughout the crowd, and the wizards released each other, looking to the west. The powerful lights over the horizon had dimmed and, with one last flare, fizzled out into the distant sky until they were no more. As the lights disappeared, darkness seemed to descend on the world.

"The barrier is gone. The Demon King is free," Balor said grimly, his face changing from sadness to anger. Chip had not noticed, but he held a staff covered with runes. Xander glanced at his brother and turned with him, facing the threat from the west together. The old wizard's face changed into a menacing countenance. At that moment, Chip could clearly see their father in both of them.

They had never looked more powerful. The students stepped

back in awe. The sons of Arkan stood side-by-side, white hair blowing in the wind, bastions of hope against the growing darkness.

"They have crossed the bridge, High Wizard," said the cleric timidly behind them, lifting his hand. Everyone turned to see what he was pointing at. The wind had picked up as if announcing a portent of doom. The sky darkened and lightning streaked. Across the front lawn, a small party of travellers had crossed the bridge, staring at the Wizard's Guild. A small boy stood before his companions, holding a little girl's hand, pointing at them.

"Han!" Chip yelled in disbelief.

Balor looked over. "What is the boy doing here?" he asked.

A feeling overcame Chip as he looked at the tiny figure of Han pointing up at him. The Guardian turned to the High Wizard.

"He is going to tell us something that will change the world."

END OF VOLUME 5.

IF YOU ENJOYED READING THIS, please leave a review on Amazon. It would be greatly appreciated.

Visit my website: www.terryironwood.com

Type your email address at the bottom of the page to be notified of my next book launch.

I have added a free short story prequel called "Weapons Master" in the upper right corner of my website. It is Garth Stone's backstory.

The Orphan's Quest audiobook with special effects is now available on Audible.

Volume Six: Stone Kingdom – Coming early November 2024

I hope you enjoyed Volume 5: Wizard's Guild. Be sure to look out for Volumes 6 and 7 of The Great Forget Fantasy Series!

The Great Forget Fantasy Series:

Volume 1: Orphan's Quest

Volume 2: Defenders of Hope

Volume 3: A Dim World

Volume 4: Guardian

Volume 5: Wizard's Guild

Volume 6: Stone Kingdom

Volume 7: Coming end of December, 2024.

Acknowledgements

I offer my heartfelt thanks to my family and friends, who provided invaluable support, wisdom, and encouragement. You know who you are. I especially want to mention Kevin C., Steve S., and Ward C., who went above and beyond.

I am delighted to work with my editor, Jason Letts from Imbue Editing, who continues to improve my writing.

Last, and certainly not least, I wish to thank an orphan, Chip, for taking me on his quest.

Many thanks,

Terry Ironwood

ABOUT THE AUTHOR

Terry Ironwood resides with his family. He holds multiple university degrees and is interested in the science of self-improvement. He is equally fascinated with physics and spirituality. Terry believes in an 'attitude of gratitude' and is grateful he can write full-time. His dream is to help others reach their full potential.

Printed in Dunstable, United Kingdom